FUGITIVE LAWMAN

Down on his luck in Chicago, Dale Carnak ends up applying for work with the Pinkerton National Detective Agency. Spotted by an old acquaintance, he is swiftly hired, and agrees to the risky assignment of infiltrating the Fraser Gang — even participating in a train robbery. But a series of misunderstandings sees Carnak become a fugitive, on the run with the rest of the outlaws. Then the bandits begin to suspect that their newest recruit is not who he claims to be . . .

JETHRO KYLE

FUGITIVE LAWMAN

Complete and Unabridged

LINFORD
Leicester

First published in Great Britain in 2014 by
Robert Hale Limited
London

First Linford Edition
published 2017
by arrangement with
Robert Hale
an imprint of
The Crowood Press
Wiltshire

A catalogue record for this book is available
from the British Library.

ISBN 978–1–4448–3523–6

Published by
F. A. Thorpe (Publishing)
Anstey, Leicestershire

Set by Words & Graphics Ltd.
Anstey, Leicestershire
Printed and bound in Great Britain by
T. J. International Ltd., Padstow, Cornwall

This book is printed on acid-free paper

1

It was a raw night in late March and the sparse fire that had been kindled from pine cones and twigs was scarcely strong enough to warm the eight men who were huddled around it, shoulder to shoulder, in a circle. When the ninth member of their party fetched up and requested room to take the chill from his own bones, the others laughed derisively and declined to move or rearrange themselves. The young man stood for a moment, as though giving them time to repent of their inhospitable manner and then said, 'Hey, you fellows, you ever seen this trick?'

The selfish men, who were refusing to budge from their comfortable positions, watched curiously as the man standing outside the circle of warmth opened a pouch fastened to his belt and took out a handful of ammunition;

maybe a dozen bright brass rifle cartridges, which gleamed in the firelight. Then he lobbed them all into the fire around which they were seated. There were cries of alarm and dismay; all eight men jumped up and ran for cover as the shells began exploding, sending bullets whistling across the little glade in which they had made their camp. When the bangs subsided, they drifted back a little shamefacedly, to find the culprit sitting at his ease before the fire, warming his hands. They voiced their opinions freely about his reckless conduct.

'What's wrong with you, man?'

'You crazy or something?'

'Bastard!'

'Cowson!'

The young man sitting on a log in front of the fire took little heed of the outraged reproaches hurled at him, remarking mildly, 'Next time I ask for a place at the fire, happen you'll let me in at once.'

This was just the sort of line that these rough and ready men understood very well and they soon forgot about the incident, holding no grudge about an impetuous action, which could easily have caused serious injury or even death. Dale Carnak, the newest recruit to the gang who had been preying on travellers across Iowa and the neighbouring states, was well aware that he needed to prove himself to the rest of them and sending those men scuttling off in fear of their lives in this way had been as good a way as any of achieving that end.

Carnak had been brought into the gang by Seth Fraser, who was the leader of the whole outfit. Fraser and his brother Dan had gone to town to check out some information appertaining to their next robbery and so in their absence discipline was more than a little slack and the boys were up to various games that the Fraser brothers would have been sure to nip in the bud, were they present. The word was that Seth and Dan had it in mind to take another train, this time one carrying a mighty haul of bullion, such as would make it possible for them all to live comfortably without undertaking any more banditry for a good long while.

'You think Seth'll be back tonight?' asked Carnak.

'Had you known him as long as some of us, you would not ask the question,' said a swarthy man to his right who always looked at Carnak as though he did not like him and suspected him of the Lord knows what, 'Those two come and go as they will. What's it to you when they get back?'

'It's nothing to me,' said Carnak, 'I was just talking.'

'You're only saying what we're all thinking,' said a man on the opposite side of the fire from Carnak, 'which is how long we're going to be stuck out here.' There were murmurs of agreement from others and Carnak felt that the general mood was in favour of his seemingly casual inquiry; for which he was exceedingly grateful.

A month earlier, Dale Carnak had

been two hundred miles away in Chicago, with no money, no job and few prospects. He had drifted to the big city in search of work, but at this time, just four years after the end of the War between the States, he was competing with a whole heap of other men in a similar case to him.

Carnak had been just nineteen when he was discharged from the army at the end of the war and since then he had wandered from city to city, state to state, taking on whatever work came along. Since 1865, he had worked as a barkeep, cowboy, faro dealer and a dozen other jobs, few of them lasting more than a month or two. Something generally came along; until now, that is. The economic depression gripping the USA at that time was like nothing anybody could recall and there always seemed to be ten men going after every job.

It had been pure chance that led him to the offices of the Pinkerton National Detective Agency. He was not alone in seeing employment with Pinkertons as offering him a helping hand out of the bind he was in. They were a big company, always taking on men. The word was that there were more Pinkerton agents in the United States at that time than there were men under arms in the Federal Army.

Be that as it may, Carnak had a stroke of luck, or so it seemed to him at the time. He was sitting on a bench among a crowd of other fellows, all hoping to work for Pinkertons and many of them, like him, looking as though they were a little down on their luck, when a smartly dressed man somewhat older than himself walked by and then stopped dead when he recognized Carnak.

'Carnak,' he cried with evident pleasure, 'As I live and breathe, it's Dale Carnak.'

It took a moment, but then he realized that the man who had hailed him in this way had served with him in the army during the war. Carnak had been only a private soldier and Chris Mitford was his sergeant. Their paths had not crossed since that time and Mitford looked as though he had done pretty well for himself over the intervening years. He drew Carnak out of the line and swiftly ushered him into his own private office.

'Well, Dale, my boy,' said Mitford, 'what's the story? You looking to work for us, that it?'

'That,' said Carnak, 'was the general idea.'

'You are one lucky devil, you know that? It is the hand of providence at work, me seeing you just then, that's all. Yes sir, providence is at work here.'

'I never had you pegged for a man who believed much in providence,' said Carnak, at which the other man let out a whoop of laughter and reached across his desk to punch him playfully on the arm.

'Here's the game and if you want to join in, then I can sign you up in our employ this very day.'

'You mean,' said Carnak slowly, 'without no interview, references or aught of that kind?'

'This here's the interview and your reference is me. What more do you want?'

It all sounded a little too pat, even for a man as desperate for work as Dale Carnak was at that point. Still and all, they say that beggars can't be choosers and it would take only another two or three days before he was a beggar indeed, being down nearly to his last dollar. That being so, Carnak accepted, sight unseen, Mitford's offer of a job, which was how he now came to be sitting round the fire here in a little wood in Iowa, posing as an outlaw.

The other eight men seated around the fire were all members of the Frasers' little gang, but they did not ride together all the time and neither did they live out in the forests and mountains in this way, except when they were on a job with the Frasers. All but Carnak had homes of their own in the country nearby and only came out on the scout like this when a job was in the wind. The rest of the time, they grubbed out their lives as farmers and stock traders.

As they sat there, chatting about this and that in a desultory fashion, one of them hushed the others, saying, 'Hark, is that hoof beats I hear?' It was indeed and some of the men reached their hands down to assure themselves that their pistols were ready and waiting. They were expecting the return of their leaders, but were also mindful of the possibility that some posse or band of vigilance men could at any time ride down upon them. Such a fate had befallen every Man-Jack of the Reno Gang not twelve months since.

They need not have been concerned, because there were only two riders and before long Seth and Dan Fraser trotted into the woodland clearing, to the relief of all those present. The brothers dismounted and strode to the fire; everybody at once moving respectfully aside to allow the two men as much access to the warmth as they might desire. There was no question of fooling around when the Frasers were present.

Seth said to Carnak, 'Well, how you doing? You got yourself acquainted with these other rascals yet?'

'Yes, I reckon,' replied Carnak, 'They been making me welcome in their own way.'

'Good, good. Now listen up, all of you. We are near the big win and if none of you boys screw up, then two weeks from now we will all be rich.'

As Chris Mitford had set out the matter back in Chicago, he was offering Carnak a chance to get into Pinkertons on the back of a fantastic success. Between the two of them, they would, leastways according to Mitford, be able to tuck away a notorious gang of train robbers. Carnak's return on the business would be securing a post at Pinkertons; no small reward, because the company were not now taking on anybody unless they chanced to have particular skills or experience, neither of which Dale Carnak happened to possess. For Mitford, there would be all the prestige of cracking the hardest case that Pinkertons was currently engaged upon. They would both come out as winners; if, that is, Mitford was to be believed. There was, inevitably, a drawback.

'Thing is, Dale,' explained Chris Mitford, 'to get close to this bunch, we need a man on the inside, someone who can tell us what they're about and where they plan to hit next.'

'You want me to get in with them, is that the way of it?'

'You got it right, straight to the point, just like you always were in the old days. Yes, if you want to work for us on a regular basis, you needs must show that you got what it takes.'

'I was thinking of something a little quieter,' said Carnak, 'just escorting strike-breakers to their work and suchlike.'

'Dale, we got a thousand men in this city will do that kind of thing. A thousand? Hell, the way the economy is right now, we got ten thousand chasing each and every job on offer here. You saw some of them out there. You would be competing for jobs with men who are older and better able than you to do work like that. I am offering you a way in round the back, like it was. Do this and your future with the Pinkerton National Detective Agency is assured. You got my oath on it.'

'What would I have to be doing?'

'First off is where you'll need a legend,' said Mitford, his face wreathed with smiles at having found the very man he needed for such a task, 'Yes sir, you are getting nowhere in an enterprise like this unless you got a legend.'

'A legend?' asked Carnak, thoroughly mystified. 'You mean like them stories from old Roman times and such?'

Mitford burst out laughing. 'Dale, you'll be the death of me. You're so fresh and green that it is a joy to listen to you. No, I ain't talking of old stories from long ago. A legend is what we in this line of work call a story that tells who you are and why you can be trusted.'

'You mean,' said Carnak thoughtfully, 'so that this bunch of robbers won't suspect I'm working for Pinkertons?'

'That's it exactly. I swear, you have a natural talent for this sort of thing. You pick up the ideas fast as can be.'

So it was that a week after this conversation, Dale Carnak found himself with a few dollars in his pocket and a room in Jacksonville, a medium-sized town in Burton county, Iowa. This town looked to the boys at Pinkertons to be at the geographical centre of the robberies and attacks that had been attributed to the nameless gang causing so much trouble in that part of the country.

Mitford had neglected to mention one small point when persuading Dale Carnak to undertake the dangerous enterprise of infiltrating the wildest bunch of outlaws to be found anywhere in the United States in that year of grace, 1869. That was that this was not the first attempt to find out somewhat about these men by setting a spy among them. Three months earlier, Pinkertons had managed to plant one of their agents on a farm just outside Jacksonville. A week after he started working there, two masked men rode up to the farm one evening, called him out and shot him down on the spot. It was because of this incident that Mitford was determined to keep his present plan strictly secret; even from everybody else working at Pinkertons. He explained to Carnak how matters stood from where he was.

'It's like this, Dale, my boy. There's so many folk working for this outfit now, all over the country, that we are sure that some of those we have took on are crooked themselves and have come to us just to find stuff out and send the information right to those we are hunting for. That being so, I am telling nobody about this operation. All the facts will be locked up in that safe of mine you see in the corner there, but nobody else in the world, bar you and me, will know that you are my man 'on the inside', as you might say.'

Had he been a little older or just a mite wiser, Dale Carnak might have seen that he had not one but two things to worry about here. The first and most obvious was that one of the gang he was trying to hitch up with might guess that he was working for Pinkertons. If that happened, his life would not be worth a wooden dime. This much, he had figured out well enough. What had not yet occurred to him, though, was that if a vigilance committee took it into their heads to hunt down these train robbers and execute summary justice upon them, then he would very likely hang alongside them. Ride with an outlaw; die with an outlaw. Such events tended in the main to be rushed and spur-of-the-moment things and if a lynch mob caught up with him while he was riding with outlaws, then his life would be forfeit. They would be most unlikely to delay the lynching so that they could wire Chicago to check up on such a wild story.

Nor was this a theoretical risk. Just three months earlier, all three of the Reno brothers had been dragged out of New Albany gaol by members of a vigilance committee known as the Scarlet Mask Society and hanged from a tree in the centre of town. They too, like the band he was seeking to join, had been preying on trains and stages. In fact, as Mitford confided to him, it was looking likely that some of the crimes attributed to the Reno brothers and their men, had really been carried out by these others.

Meanwhile, at the camp outside Jacksonville, Seth Fraser laid out his ideas for the big operation, which he reckoned would mean that all of them could rest easy for a space without worrying about money for the foreseeable future. As he and his brother told the tale, it was simplicity itself.

'Here's the way of it,' said Seth to the listening men. 'You boys might know that there is a new mint in Carson City, way out in Nevada. There's a heap of silver being dug up there and turned into coins. Most of those silver coins are coming east on the Central Pacific to Chicago. First big consignment's coming in fifteen days.'

'How much?' asked one of the men.

'How much? You wouldn't guess how much, so I'll tell you. Just under a hundred thousand.'

There were exclamations of surprise and a few low whistles of amazement. 'God almighty,' said somebody. 'That works out at . . . well, a hell of a lot each.'

Dan Fraser, who was by nature a deal more taciturn than his brother, said, 'A hell of a lot is right. It comes out at about ten thousand for every one of us.'

'Ten thousand? Shit, we'll be set up for life,' said somebody else. 'I never heard tell of such a thing.'

Seth said, 'Still, like it says in the cookbook, 'first catch your hare'. I'll show you men how me and Dan have gauged this.'

Dan added at this point, 'Yes, you listen good to what my brother tells you now. Before God, any man here screws this up for us and I will cut out his liver and eat it.' When Dan Fraser made such promises they sounded less like flowery and exaggerated figures of speech and more like a man casually mentioning what he would have for supper that day. The excited buzz of conversation stopped at once and there was dead silence while Seth reasoned out the matter to them.

'You're all knowing the last time we robbed a train, we done it by night. But that old red lantern trick is wearing awful thin now and I don't think it will answer for this job. Not to mention where that train is due to pass by the area where we will hit it in broad daylight, at maybe ten in the morning. No, we'll try something new this time.'

One of the men was incautious enough to interrupt at this point, asking what this new thing might be that they would be trying, whereupon Seth Fraser said irritably, 'If you'll just keep your mouth closed, you damned whore's son, then you might find out. We are going to set a mine.'

Nobody else dared to ask what was meant by this surprising statement, figuring that Seth would tell them in his own good time.

'Here's the lay of the land. I have ten pounds of fine-grained powder, which I purpose to set off as the train approaches. We'll do it so the driver sees the explosion and knows he must stop, on account of the tracks being all blowed up. When he stops, out we ride and take what we will.'

Dan Fraser chipped in, saying, 'The long and the short of it is, you all go back to your homes for two weeks and then we meet up the day before the train passes north of here. There'd best not be a heap of foolish questions, for I reckon my brother here has told all that is needful.'

What it amounted to was that the eight of them had been summoned from their homes at short notice to come all the way out here and were now being dismissed again; all on the whim of the Frasers. They all reacted to this turn of events stoically, for which there were two good reasons.

In the first place, riding with the Frasers was a profitable business, as the two brothers had an almost supernatural knack for knowing where and when large amounts of money or precious metal were being transported by road and rail. The small holdings and farms on which those men lived produced only a fraction of the amount of money that they obtained by working under the direction of Seth and Dan Fraser. This provided a powerful incentive for biting their tongues when the Frasers behaved in such a high-handed fashion. Those who did not like the way that Seth and Dan ran the operation did not need to stay with them.

The second reason for remaining silent if one was vexed with either Seth or Dan Fraser was that both men had a disturbing habit of shooting out of hand any man careless enough to get crosswise to them. Displaying anger and setting yourself in opposition to either of the Fraser brothers was next door to putting a gun to your head and blowing out your brains.

2

Getting in with the Fraser Gang had, in the end, been ridiculously and disconcertingly easy. Dale had been advanced enough money by Mitford to set him up in a cheap boarding house in Jacksonville. The idea was that he would then try to hook up with the Frasers or some member of their gang. Pinkertons had a strong notion that Seth Fraser was running the operation, but most nobody in Barlow County had the least notion of this. Both the Frasers were tolerably well known in and around Jacksonville, not as criminals, but rather as well-to-do businessmen. Not that anybody seemed to know for sure what their business entailed; just that whatever it was, the two men always had enough money to throw around when they came to town.

Attempting to strike up an acquaintance with a band of desperados and killers looked likely to be a damned tricky undertaking and if Dale Carnak had not been nigh at the point at which he would soon be starving, then he would most likely not have engaged to do it. But there, he was desperate and perhaps Mitford had sensed this. In the event, the matter had been as simple as falling off a log.

The first night he fetched up in Jacksonville, Dale drifted into the Broken Arrow saloon to ask around. Despite Mitford's apparent confidence in him, he had not the faintest idea how to go about the thing and, naïve as he was, he was still all too well aware that asking too many questions about such dangerous characters as the Frasers and their men would not be a healthy course of action to follow. All that Mitford could tell him was that Seth and Dan Fraser were almost certainly behind this gang and if he could pick up with them on friendly terms, why then, it might lead somewhere.

Seth Fraser had a reputation not only

as being a fairly wealthy man, but also one that you crossed at your peril. On the first evening that Dale Carnak turned up at the Broken Arrow, Seth Fraser had just delivered an expert beating to a fellow he had accused of jumping the line at the bar. To be fair to the man, Fraser always expected to be served next as soon as he signalled that his glass was empty and it was this fellow's misfortune to have objected when he saw the barkeep heading towards Fraser, when he himself had already been standing there for some minutes before Fraser had even approached the bar.

The fight had been pretty one-sided, and the other party had not even been able to get in a single blow. Although both he and Fraser had been heeled, neither had gone for their weapons; feeling that a simple trading of heavy blows met the present case. After he had beaten the man to the ground, Fraser had gone a little far by kicking him up the backside and telling him to leave the saloon on all fours. It was the final and unnecessary humiliation which came within a whisker of costing Seth Fraser his very life.

Carnak knew nothing of all this when he entered the Broken Arrow that Saturday night. As he walked into the place a fellow pushed past him roughly, from behind. He turned to reprove this man for his discourtesy, only to see him take out a pistol and draw down on a man at the bar. Without even thinking, Carnak knocked the man's arm up as he fired, causing the ball to shatter the huge looking-glass above the bar, rather than embedding itself in the back of the man who had been the original target. Carnak followed up by twisting the man's arm and depriving him of the pistol.

Once those in the bar had recovered from their surprise, a number of them fell upon the man who had fired the shot and dragged him outside. He was recognized as the man with whom Fraser had had the altercation and it was quickly realized that this young man had prevented Seth Fraser from being shot in the back. And this is how Dale Carnak was, in the most natural way imaginable, enabled to make the acquaintance of the gang leader.

A few days later, 2 April 1869 edition of *The Jacksonville and Bartlow County Intelligencer and Weekly Record* carried the following piece about this incident:

On the 28th ultimo the patrons of that renowned drinking hole, the BROKEN ARROW, were shocked and distressed when a foolish and intoxicated fellow attempted to exact sanguinary vengeance upon our local entrepreneur, SETH FRASER. The cowardly stranger shot at Mr FRASER's back and might have succeeded in this dastardly assassination, were it not for a young stranger who, at no small risk to his own life, disarmed the assailant. Several able-bodied drinkers then took the would-be ambush-killer outside and endeavoured with great vigour to show him that such tricks as shooting a man in the back will not be tolerated in BARTLOW COUNTRY. Say what you will about some of the rougher elements in our corner of the state, but the so-called Rattlesnake Code rules supreme and no man is apt to be shot down without first being offered a chance to defend himself!

Part of the 'legend' that Chris Mitford had put together for Carnak consisted of circulating his name to the sheriff's office in Jacksonville as somebody to be on the alert for. The relationship between Pinkertons and the official agencies of the law were at that time so blurred that it was hard for some to tell whether or not Pinkertons agents had the same authority as regular peace officers. Alan Pinkerton, the founder, encouraged this confusion; when first set up, he called his company the North-Western Police Agency. A title like that was liable, to say the least of it, to create confusion in the minds of many as to whether or not the men from this agency were police officers or private individuals.

US marshals and sheriffs seemed to share this confusion, at least to some extent, because they passed on a lot of information to Pinkertons and received in return whatever tips that Pinkertons felt able to share with them. This was done by means of a regular leaflet sent to various offices, warning of unsavoury characters who might be heading in their direction.

A week before Dale Carnak arrived in Jacksonville, the sheriff's office in that town received in the mail a circular from Pinkertons in Chicago, giving the names and descriptions of a half dozen lawless types who might be heading to Iowa from other states. One of these read:

Dale Carnak

Age 24. Height 5 feet 10 inches. Weight 126 pounds. Light hair, blue eyes and even features. The above, who also goes by the name of Chuck Mellors, Dave Starr and Dave Cardew, is known to have engaged in road-agent work in Kansas and is also suspected of having been involved in robbing a train in that state, along with others. Thought to be heading North West. No warrants or rewards, but bears watching.

Chris Mitford had thought this a right cunning move. The way that the Frasers seemed to both know the best targets for their depredations and also escape notice, suggested to the people at Pinkertons that they must have inside information of some sort; maybe a corrupt deputy or even sheriff. If so, then circulating Dale Carnak's name in this way would be giving him a testimonial if he was lucky enough to get to know either of the Fraser brothers.

When Seth Fraser first met Carnak

in the saloon the night that the younger man saved his life, he had not yet seen this faked reference, but took to Carnak quite naturally. He did not fail to observe that this was a young man who was a little cagy about his past; where he was from and where he was going. He first gave his name as Dave, but then after a few drinks, confided that his real name was Dale; Dale Carnak. Fraser was definitely interested. His 'gang' was not a static body of men with a fixed number of members. Sometimes the Frasers talked over the behaviour of some man or another and came to the conclusion that he was more of a liability than an asset and this or that fellow would accordingly be dropped. At other times, some likely man would pop up and the Frasers would invite him to join them in some enterprise.

A few days after first meeting Seth Fraser, Carnak chanced to bump into him on Main Street. Fraser was pleasant and talkative. He said, 'I was reading about you just yesterday. You are a regular one for modesty!'

'Reading about me? Where?'

'That don't signify,' said Fraser, lowering his voice. 'Seems like you might be the sort of fellow I have been looking for.'

'For what? I'm not looking for a steady job or anything of that sort.'

'No, so it seems. Is it true that you have been mixed up in robbing a train?'

'Who told you so?' said Carnak indignantly, 'I wasn't arrested or nothing of that sort.'

'I wouldn't be wanting to offer you work if you had. Those as are taken by the law are what you might call the losers in the game I run.'

'Meaning?'

'Meaning, if you are looking for some good money in exchange for a day's work, then right now is the time to speak out.'

'Yeah,' said Carnak, 'I reckon I am at that. Leastways, I am if this 'work' does not signify wielding a shovel or pick.'

Fraser laughed out loud at that. 'No,'

he said, 'It is nothing in the agricultural line.'

All of which led to Carnak meeting eight other members of the Fraser brothers' little team out in the pine woods beyond the town. Having now a date and rough location for the Frasers' next piece of work, he needed to convey this information to Mitford up in Chicago. Since the end of the war, no telegraph office would take any message in code or phrased in any language other than English. There was the fear that some conspirators might try to use the telegraph wires to coordinate an uprising against the military rule of the defeated southern states and so all cables, throughout the entire country, had to be in plain English. Carnak and Mitford had devised a simple system to bypass this restriction and the day after he got back to Jacksonville after his sojourn in the forest, he went to the telegraph office and sent the following message to a telegraphic address in Chicago:

My horse Silver has been travelling a lot by road and rail. We came from home, Mr Carson from the city joined us on a vacation. April is the twelfth month I train Silver and he will look and be fine. He jumped hedges and 20 fences, rode for miles to the north and south of country around Jacksonville.

The clerk thought this a wordy and needlessly expensive sort of message to send, but it was nothing to him if this young fellow wanted to throw his money round in this fashion and he sent off the message without any problem.

The office where the message ended up was one of Pinkertons' cover addresses; somewhere that cables and letters could be sent without it being obvious that they were heading for Pinkertons. An hour after it arrived, a boy was dispatched to the head office to pass the apparently mundane wire on to Chris Mitford, who read it with enormous satisfaction. The trap was laid.

The code that Mitford and Carnak had agreed upon was rudimentary, but none the less effective for that. It entailed simply writing a passage so that every third word conveyed the message and the rest were just fillers. In the present case, the decoded text read:

Silver travelling by rail from Carson City on 12 April train will be jumped 20 miles north of Jacksonville.

Everything was now in place. Mitford had almost two weeks to prepare for his great coup and he didn't aim to make any errors about it either.

Having a man who would, he assumed, actually be riding with the bandits, was all that he could have hoped. The fact that Dale Carnak was almost certainly a dead man did not cause any stirrings of regret in Mitford's heart; his conscience was not that tender. Carnak had been keen enough to take the job and it was up to him now to look to his own skin. When the shooting started, it was highly

34

likely that a number on the outlaws' side of the battle would be lying dead when the smoke cleared. But still and all, he had never really cared overmuch for Carnak, even when they were fighting in the same unit of the Union Army. All things considered, his death would simplify matters and prevent word getting out at a later stage as to how this trick had been pulled. That would be a bonus as well, because if this scheme worked once, it could work twice. Which might not be the case if some fool who knew about the mechanics of the thing was shooting his mouth off about it later. All things taken together, Dale Carnak's death would be a most desirable outcome from this operation, ensuring, if nothing else, that Chris Mitford would not have to share the glory of the thing with anybody else.

Seth Fraser didn't seem to want anything to do with Carnak until closer to the time of the robbery and so he had the better part of two weeks to think things over and try to work out the best move. As he lay on his bed in the boarding house after sending the wire to Mitford, some of the less obvious disadvantages of his position began to occur to him. If Fraser had reason to suppose that he, Dale Carnak, was a crook, then presumably the law would be under the same misapprehension. Which was likely to leave him in a damned awkward situation if anything went wrong and Pinkertons were not on the scene to vouch for him.

It was at this point that Carnak suddenly asked himself how much of this setup was Pinkertons and how much was a private venture of Chris Mitford's. Did anybody apart from Mitford even know of his presence here? Was he actually working for Pinkertons at all? Suppose, at a later stage, Mitford denied knowing Carnak; what sort of stew would that leave him in?

Dale Carnak was not a deep thinker, but he was a thorough one. After somewhat above an hour's solid reasoning, he had come up with a pile of dangers to himself that had not before occurred to him. He considered the notion of cutting and running right then, but then he would be in no better a case than he had been when first he arrived in Chicago; that is to say, penniless and lacking money, work and a place to live. No, at least for the time being, he would go along with the path fate seemed to have set out for him, but he was going to be a mite sharper from here on in about setting mind to his own interests and welfare. He might still come out on top here, but he would need to tread very carefully.

* * *

The Frasers were twins, although fraternal rather than identical. They were thirty-six years old at this time, which meant that they had reached a far greater age than many outlaws managed. They had done this by not being overly greedy and leaving a certain time between their robberies. This was one of the reasons that they had lasted so long. The other was that they were not vainglorious and in the game to become renowned gun-slingers, the way that a lot of outlaws were. They did not have a hankering to read about the exploits of 'The Fraser Gang' in the newspapers, nor have every-body think them the most daring fellows to walk the earth since the Devil was a boy. All they wanted was a steady supply of easy money.

Seth and Dan still lived in their childhood home; a stone-built farm-house some miles south of Jacksonville. They had neither of them ever married and in fact still lived with their ma, who was, these days, confined to her bed. In the past, the two men had left their home for periods of up to a year, but had always returned. This tow had prevented them from being captured; the fact that so many of their crimes had been committed in other states, as far away as Texas and Arizona. As they had grown older, though, they some-how seemed to prefer to live here on the farm where they had grown up, with the reassuring and familiar presence of their mother in the background.

Old Mrs Fraser had ruled that house with her iron and indomitable will from time out of mind; certainly as long as her two sons could recall. Even now, with the old lady not having moved from her bedroom for these two years or more, she still succeeded in keeping everything under her own control. There were four servants in the house alongside Mrs Fraser and her 'boys' and all four of them lived in terror of the old woman. So, surprisingly, did Seth and Dan. They might be the very Devil incarnate when throwing their weight about in the Jacksonville saloons, but they were a real pair of lambs when it came to dealings with their mother.

By her bed was propped a silver-headed, ebony cane and if Mrs Fraser wanted attention, she would reach out and bang that cane on the floor. Whoever heard that rapping had best move up those stairs right smartly or the old lady would know the reason for the delay. Sometimes it was one of the servants who rushed up to attend to her; at other times one or the other of her sons, who she still scolded and reproved as though they were ten or eleven years of age.

It's impossible to say how much old Mrs Fraser guessed about her son's business. Like as not, she knew the whole story of their doings, although they had never spoken openly to her of how they made their livelihood. It was just that ever since they were youngsters, their mother always knew what they had been up to, without anybody apparently telling her. It was downright scary sometimes, like she was a witch or something and could see in a crystal ball what they had been doing when out of her sight. They would come back from fishing on some neighbour's land and their mother was there at the kitchen door ready to upbraid and sometimes whip them. They had neither of them ever been able to conceal the least misdemeanour from her.

After Seth and Dan had been up to wish their mother goodnight, they came down and sat smoking in companionable silence for a spell, before Seth said, 'What do you think to the new fellow?'

'Carnak? He will do well enough. Why?'

'We don't know aught about him, bar what Pinkertons sent to the sheriff. You think it a true bill?'

'I reckon. We can drop him if you'd sooner.'

'No, I'm just asking your view. We needs must start work soon on fixing up that mine,' said Seth, 'We must be sure it is made real good.'

'With ten pounds of powder, I can't see how it can fail.'

3

On Tuesday morning, Chris Mitford received a summons from the great man himself. Alan Pinkerton wished him to attend at his earliest convenience and when Mr Pinkerton himself deigned to send you such a message, you had best look lively and ensure that your earliest convenience coincided with his.

Pinkerton was coming up to fifty, but there was not a spare ounce of flesh on him and he looked as healthy as a man half his age. His early life in Glasgow had been hard and he had spent the first years of his adulthood as a cooper or barrel-maker. Looking at him in that plush office of his, you had the impression that he would still be a formidable man to face up to in a fist fight. His voice was gravelly and rough, with a Scots accent you could draw a knife through.

'Ah, Mitford, come in, laddie and draw up yon chair.'

Chris Mitford might be a tough man and a bit of a bully into the bargain in his own department, but in front of Mr Pinkerton himself, he behaved like an office boy who has been caught out pocketing the petty cash. Pinkerton was aware of the effect that his overpowering personality had upon those who worked for him and did his best to set the man at ease. 'Ach, dinna fret. You're not in trouble. I'm just wanting to know about this train robbery business away over in Iowa. Your information is sound?'

'Yes sir, I believe so.'

'Ye believe so? Or know so? Which is it?'

'I know it's sound, sir.'

Pinkerton filled and lit his pipe. Then he said, 'D'ye have somebody on the inside, is that the way of it?'

For a fraction of a second, Mitford had the opportunity of coming clean and explaining his strategy in the case.

The only thing is, the more he had thought about it, the more he realized that at the end of the affair, the man who had risked his life to infiltrate the Fraser Gang might well be viewed as more heroic and deserving of praise than he himself. It wouldn't do; he needed all the credit for breaking up those train robbers and so he said with barely the slightest hesitation, 'No sir, nothing like that. It is based upon facts which an informant has passed to me.'

Alan Pinkerton stared for a moment or two at his subordinate, wondering whether or not he should press for further and fuller particulars of the precise way in which the unlikable man seated in front of him had come by his facts. He decided against it. 'I'll tell ye this for nothing,' he said to Mitford, 'crack this case and you are heading to the very top here. The ordinary lawmen are closing in on the Frasers, although as yet they don't even know their names. But it can't be long. I want us to be the ones who catch those men and

44

put a stop to their activities. Ye hear me, Mitford? Don't be letting me down, now.'

When he left the interview with his boss, two things were crystal clear in Mitford's mind. One was that if he cracked this and put a stop to the Fraser brothers, then his career with Pinkertons would be unstoppable. The other was that having to all intents and purposes told a direct lie to the old man himself, he had better make damned sure that it never came to light that all along he did have an inside man in the gang. Alan Pinkerton had been known to turn a blind eye to many peccadillos, but he never tolerated anybody lying to his face. If that came out, then Chris Mitford would be finished.

* * *

The days crawled by for Dale Carnak in Jacksonville. He was not a man who took that much to his own company and had never been one for reading or other entertainments. So it was that he started taking long walks in the hills around Jacksonville, thinking as he walked about the setup he was in and trying to fathom out the wisest course of action to protect his own best interests.

Eventually, the time wore away until it was 11 April and the robbery was only twenty-four hours away. Carnak got up that day and, before leaving his room, checked that the army Colt, which he had carried at his hip for better than five years now, was loaded and ready. He spun the cylinder, cocked and dry fired it a few times, until he was perfectly happy with the way the mechanism was running.

Seth Fraser had told Carnak to be ready to ride out by about noon that day; the idea being that they would meet up with everybody else, just a short way out of town. One of the ways that the Frasers had prevented their own names being associated with a 'gang' or anything else of that sort, was by making sure that nobody ever saw them alongside a bunch of armed men riding around and kitted out as if they were going to war. His boys met up out in the woods and then after the action, they dispersed to their homes without any fuss and bother. There was none of the foolish swaggering around and showing off in towns that had been the downfall of so many other bands of robbers. Half the time, that sort of man was more concerned with making an exhibition of himself and posing as a hard man than he was with the practical gains of the enterprise. For the Frasers, robbery with violence was strictly a business and they only worked with men who felt the same way.

For the present operation, the idea was that the men would assemble and then ride north towards the Central Pacific railroad line heading up to Chicago. They would then camp out not far from the line and be ready to strike when the train came by at about ten in the morning. The point that the

Frasers had chosen was flat ground and you could see clear to the horizon. This was important, because the aim was to cause the train to halt, rather than derail it. Seth and Dan wanted the driver to see the explosion ahead of him and put on the brakes. The eleven riders would then move in and help themselves to the contents of the special van.

The other men greeted Carnak affably enough when he arrived. They seemed disposed to treat him as one of them and he felt sure that his little trick of throwing the ammunition into the fire that night had helped this along a bit. They perhaps felt that he was not a man to be trifled with.

When once they were all arrived, Dan Fraser addressed them thus: 'We are riding twenty miles now and do not want to look like a body of men set on mischief. Which means we will leave in ones and twos at intervals of fifteen minutes. My brother will leave first and then wait on the road and direct those as come after to where we will be camping. Try to look like ordinary civilians.'

Dan Fraser was a man of few words, but those he spoke he expected to have notice taken of. Everything went smoothly and the party left at intervals, with most of their weaponry concealed.

While the Frasers were busy organizing the robbery of the train from Carson City, with a view to stealing the silver it was carrying, two other bands of men were setting out to prevent them from doing that very thing. Pinkertons were absolutely determined to catch the gang before the official law and this looked to be their best chance. Their plans were the most detailed and specific, because of course they knew, via Chris Mitford — and Dale Carnak — just when and where the theft was to occur.

Some ten miles west of where the ambush of the train was planned to take place, was a little junction. It was called Barnard's Crossing and trains stopped there to take on water and sometimes passengers. The day before the train from out west was due through, this spot was a regular hive of activity. Mitford was throwing his weight around to no small extent and was in charge of fourteen agents from Chicago; every one of whom was armed to the teeth with the most modern and up-to-date rifles. These men were standing around at Barnard's Crossing next to a railroad carriage, which was parked on a little line leading off from the junction. Mitford was marching round, doing his best to see that everything would go smoothly the next day. He said to the half dozen men sitting and smoking near the carriage, 'You boys know what you got to do?'

'Sure,' said one of the group, who was something of a joker, 'We wait 'til this here carriage is hitched up to the train, then we bust open our weapons, move down to the end van and rob the bullion.'

Mitford glared balefully at him.

'Don't screw around with me, you hear what I tell you? I'm going to be mighty pissed at any of you fellows as fouls this up. Now I'll ask again, you all know what's what?'

There were hurried murmurs of assent. They were looking forward to the action the next day, which promised to be like shooting fish in a barrel.

Mitford went along to another huddle of men and called one of them over to him. This man, he led out of earshot of the others. 'You know we're not going to be issuing a challenge or anything in the morning?' he said.

'Meaning, we just shoot when they are close enough? Yeah, I'm easy with that.'

'There will be a young fellow with the gang. He's only twenty-four.' He gave a good description of Dale Carnak. 'It would ease my mind greatly if that fellow was to get shot first and not wounded neither. Do I make myself plain?'

'I reckon,' said the other laconically. 'You want him killed.'

'Yes, I thought we could speak openly,' said Mitford. 'You deal with that man and I'll stand friend to you and aid your career with us.'

'Sounds good,' said the man and then walked off to rejoin his companions.

The Pinkerton boys were not the only bunch who were intent on protecting that silver. The sheriff of the nearest town between Barnard's Crossing and Chicago had his own ideas on the case and unknown to Pinkertons had summoned up a posse to patrol the Central Pacific line as it passed through his jurisdiction. It didn't need the greatest mind of the age to see that a train carrying a hundred thousand in silver coin might be a tempting target to those preying on the railroads.

★ ★ ★

When everybody had arrived at the spot that the Frasers had chosen as a camping ground, Seth took the opportunity to deliver a little homily.

'I don't want any fooling around here tonight. No drinking strong liquor or aught of that sort. Once it is dark, I'll take one of you across over to the line and we'll lay the mine. I want it buried good, so if some damned busybody passes by, nothing'll notice.'

The men settled down in the wooded slope overlooking the railroad at a distance of perhaps a mile. There was some casual conversation, which centred mostly around what each of them would do with ten thousand dollars. Once darkness had blanketed the hillside, Seth Fraser came over to where Carnak was sitting, his mind running over how he would play things in the morning.

'Carnak, you come with me. You're a young fellow and won't make heavy weather of a bit of digging.'

The two men walked down the slope to where the railroad line cut across the landscape. Carnak carried an entrenching tool and Fraser a keg of powder with a length of fuse trailing from it. As they walked, Fraser explained how it would be in the morning. 'I aim to light the fuse on this thing,' he said, holding up the little wooden keg, 'just as soon as we catch a sight of that there train. I calculate it will take precisely one minute to blow.'

'And that'll give the driver time enough to stop?'

'I reckon so. We'll wait up yonder and then ride down soon as the mine is sprung.'

It took Carnak only ten minutes to scrape a hole about a foot deep, right beneath one of the rails. Seth Fraser packed rocks around the wooden keg and then filled any spaces with pebbles. Then he piled loose earth into the rest of the spaces, being careful to smooth it all down and make the area around the hole look just like the surrounding ground. When he'd finished, the only clue that there was anything amiss was provided by the long white fuse. This he tucked neatly under the rail. Unless somebody was down on all fours, it would be impossible to tell that there was anything wrong.

'What if it rains tonight?' asked Carnak.

'I don't look for rain,' said Fraser briefly. 'We had best get back and sleep. I want you all up at dawn; there's no place in my outfit for slug-a-beds.'

As he lay there under the stars, trying to sleep, Dale Carnak found himself unable to work things out in his mind; even to his own satisfaction. Was he really working for Pinkertons? Could he consider himself a bona fide lawman now or was this all part of some strange initiation ceremony or test? The harder he had been turning matters over in recent days, the less he trusted Chris Mitford. He did not have much choice other than to accept this offer of work, but a horrible fear was coming upon him that there wasn't really a job at all and that after this little adventure was over, Mitford would give him the bum's rush and that would be that. If that were really the case, why should he not just stick with the Frasers and take his cut of the loot?

Carnak rebelled against this venial and crooked notion. No, by God, he had been engaged to work for a law enforcement agency and that is exactly what he was going to do. Damn Chris Mitford! As far as Carnak was concerned, he had been given a job to do and it entailed helping to put a stop to the larcenous activities of the Fraser brothers. He had always lived his life straight as a die, at least according to his own lights, and he was not about to take the outlaw trail at this stage. No, he would stick with it and behave as though he were a genuine Pinkerton's agent, see where that led him.

Unbeknown to the Frasers and their gang, the posse of men from the little town of Claremont were camped out barely three miles from them. There were eight of them and apart from the sheriff and his deputy, all the rest were there only for the profit of the thing. They were getting daily expenses for riding out like this and were also promised a share of any reward money that should turn up. Since that sort of cash normally entailed the clause of 'dead or alive', these men were very likely to shoot first and reason things out later. They had no special animosity towards the gang that had been robbing trains along this way, but every one of them could surely do with a little extra money. If they were not actually bounty hunters, then it was a close-run thing. Their interest in justice began and ended with the possible benefits to their own personal finances.

4

The Frasers went round their campsite, prodding men with their boots and occasionally kicking them in order to get them up and moving. 'Come on, you lazy sons of bitches,' said Dan Fraser, 'that damned train will be in Chicago before you bastards have opened your eyes.'

'What's the rush?' asked one of them men incautiously. 'We got at least another four hours afore it shows here.'

'You stupid cowson,' said Seth, 'you know that for a fact, do you? I want to be down there by the track, ready and waiting at least two hours 'fore that train is due. And I want you boys prepared to ride out at the self-same time. Jesus Christ almighty, there's a hundred thousand at stake here and all you fools can think of is another five minutes' sleep.'

At this point, Dan Fraser chipped in, saying, 'Just recall what I told you men. God help anybody who screws this up. You hear me, now?'

Nobody felt disposed to quarrel with the Frasers and so all of them got up, stamped about to warm themselves up a little and began checking their guns and horses, so that they would be ready for action at a moment's notice.

The Pinkerton's men over at Barnard's Crossing were rousing themselves at that same early hour. Mitford was edgy; ready and willing to kick anybody's arse if it would speed things up by so much as a second and make the success of this enterprise assured. Everything was riding on this game. Alan Pinkerton had intimated to him that he found the presence, within a few hundred miles of his head-quarters, of an active and ruthless gang of train robbers to be mighty embarrassing and next door to a personal affront.

If Mitford was able to sort out this business and put a stop to the robberies, then he would be the great man's blue-eyed boy; at least for some while to come. If he fouled it up, though, his fall from grace would be swift and he would most likely be finished at Pinkertons.

The arrangement for the ambush was a simple one. The trap was a special carriage that would be tacked on the train, right next to the van carrying the silver.

The train that was heading towards Barnard's Crossing was a regular passenger service, with a van added at the back, just in front of the guard's van right at the back of the train. When the train reached the junction where the Pinkerton's men were waiting, the guard's van and the carriage with the bullion would be uncoupled from the train and their carriage would be placed next to that containing the silver from Carson City. This special coach of theirs was reinforced with metal plates and would be all but impregnable to bullets. Even the windows were boarded up, with only narrow slits for the rifles to poke out of.

The plan could hardly be more straightforward. The train would travel down the tracks in the direction of Chicago. If, as Mitford knew very well would be the case, it proved to be a prize that the Fraser brothers could not keep their hands off, then when they rode down, the Pinkerton's men would be waiting for them in that armoured carriage. It would be a massacre; the men on horseback could be picked off just like they were targets at a carnival shooting gallery.

The posse from Claremont did not rise at dawn nor anything like it. Even the sheriff had been drinking heavily the night before and it was closer to nine than eight by the time they finally began to stir. Half the men had dull headaches from being so liquored up and there was a general reluctance to get up and start moving. The boys insisted first on brewing up some coffee and sat there for over half an hour, exchanging remarks such as, 'Hey, that poteen is really something!' and 'My mouth feels like the floor of a cowshed!' and similar pointless statements. The sheriff was growing more angered by the minute as the time approached for the arrival of the train from Carson City.

Seth Fraser consulted the massive gold hunter whose substantial chain swung from the front of his waistcoat. The watch was the only outward display of wealth that he allowed himself. Flashing your money around was a sure-fire way of getting folks jealous and setting them to asking where a body got all his money from. 'It's nine,' he announced. 'I am going down to the tracks now and as soon as I am gone, I want all you boys to break camp and be standing ready and waiting besides your horses. And them saddled up, too, and raring to go. Dan, you'll make it sure?'

'Yeah. Just get going now. I'll set a watch for any laggards here, you have no fear on it.'

The nine men were not best pleased to learn that they were expected to stand to, next to their mounts for an hour or more, doing nothing. Still, there are some men who one feels that one can express irritation to about an annoying proposal of this type and then again, there are others around whom you feel it is wise to keep silent when you feel that way. The Fraser brothers fell very definitely into that second category and there were no murmurs of discontent or annoyance to be heard as they set to and saddled up their horses.

The train from Carson City puffed into Barnard's Crossing within a few minutes of its expected arrival. While the locomotive took on water, the guard's van and strong-room carriage were uncoupled and when the engine was all filled up, the points were changed and the train backed up onto the siding and picked up the armoured carriage of the Pinkerton's men. Then it went forward again and reversed back to take on the guard's van and carriage containing the bullion.

While these manoeuvres were in progress, passengers started leaning out of the window and asking what the hell was going on. The sudden reversing of the train had taken some by surprise and there was some irritation at the unexpected jolting that they had received.

When the operation was completed, the Pinkerton's men boarded their carriage, leaving one man behind at Barnard's Crossing to take care of the horses. Then the locomotive's whistle blew and they were away.

* * *

While he waited patiently beside his horse, Dale Carnak fell to thinking; which was by way of being an uncommon activity for him. Something had been nagging away at his mind for the last day or so and he could not think what it might be. Then, in a flash, it came to him and he blinked in astonishment, amazed that the weak point in this plan had not before come to the forefront of his mind like this. According to the Frasers, they would all of them be carrying away some ten thousand dollars as a share of the spoils. This was in silver coins, though, not gold bars. Each of those silver dollars must weigh about an ounce, say. Carnak was not a whale on ciphering and figure work, but he knew that there was sixteen ounces to a pound. He further knew that doubling sixteen gave you thirty-two and that there were about three lots of thirty-two in a hundred. That meant that a hundred dollars in silver would weigh in at around six pounds. A thousand dollars would be sixty pounds and ten thousand must weigh around six hundredweight.

Now, the Frasers had told them to bring roomy saddle-bags with them, but their horses were not likely to be able to travel far with a rider and an additional six hundred pounds in weight. Not that a leather saddle-bag would hold anything like that amount, anyway.

Carnak knew that he was not himself

possessed of the sharpest mind in the world, but he had assumed that the Frasers were bright ones. It gradually dawned upon him as he stood there, that they too might not be great shakes in the calculating department and had not thought through the actual figures and weights involved in this present project. He wondered if he should speak out, but did not wish to draw attention to himself by appearing to have been thinking too deeply. He decided to keep his own counsel.

★ ★ ★

It was ten before the posse from Claremont was ready to move out. As Sheriff Palmer remarked to his deputy, the damned train would be in Chicago by the time those bastards were ready to ride. This, he reflected bitterly, was the problem with raising a party of this sort to support you. They were keen as mustard to collect their daily allowance and were first in line for a share in any reward money, but when it came to actually doing anything to earn the money, that was a different matter. At least, though, these men looked like they would be able to shoot, if the occasion demanded it. That, thankfully, was something.

* * *

Seth Fraser was sitting by the railroad tracks with his hand resting lightly upon one rail. He wasn't a Red Indian, but he could tell by the faint trembling of the steel when a train was some miles off. He felt that slight fluttering beneath his fingertips now and took out the box of lucifers. Then he unfolded the fuse from where he had tucked it beneath the rail and waited until the train was in plain view.

* * *

There was too much good-humoured banter floating around the carriage for

Mitford's liking. Since this was likely to be a regular turkey shoot, with them firing from cover against a bunch of riders, the Pinkerton's men did not anticipate any personal danger. Mitford saw a man poke his rifle playfully out of one of the firing ports and he cursed at the fellow. 'Put that goddamned weapon back inside. We don't want to frighten those boys away. They're not supposed to be knowing about us.'

The man looked a little crestfallen and quickly withdrew his rifle into the darkened carriage.

'Seems to me,' said Mitford irritably, 'some of you boys have got shit for brains. Just keep looking out of the ports now on both sides and be ready for trouble when it comes.'

* * *

As soon as Seth Fraser saw the train in the distance, he lit the fuse of the mine, which at once began to fizz and splutter. Then he jumped up, mounted his horse and galloped back up the slope to where the others were waiting. By the time he reached them, he knew that something had gone terribly wrong. It took him a good three minutes to reach the woods and yet the mine was supposed to have blown after only a minute. He began cursing, softly at first and then with increasing vehemence as the seconds ticked away and it became obvious that the mine was not about to explode. By the time he came to the others, who were mustered among the trees and looking down anxiously towards the railroad, he was gripped by a paroxysm of fury. Even his brother Dan dared not ask whether things had miscarried.

The eleven men stared in dumb anguish as the train carrying their hundred thousand dollars thundered along the tracks and looked as though it was about to rumble out of their lives forever, taking their fortunes with it. It was a bitter blow.

The fuse had not wholly died; the

flame had flickered and jerked along the cord until a fraction of an inch before it reached the powder keg. At that point, for some inexplicable reason, it had sputtered and died. Not altogether, though. The cord still glowed a sullen red, but it was fading and the spark of heat was all but extinguished. As the locomotive rumbled over it, however, the fuse shifted slightly and the flame suddenly flared into life again and leapt along the fuse. The train had almost passed before the burning fuse touched off Seth Fraser's mine.

The Frasers and their men were all gazing gloomily at the train as it passed, having resigned themselves to the fact that the robbery had failed. But just when it looked like they would be leaving the scene penniless, there was a mighty roar and the rear end of the train disappeared in a flash of light. 'Well, boys,' said Seth, 'we might yet be in business!'

The explosion of the ten pounds of fine-grained powder took place directly beneath the carriage containing Mitford and his men. The sides of the carriage might have been plated with steel, but the floor was only wood. The force of the explosion tore up through the carriage, killing eight of the men immediately, including Mitford himself. The others were stunned by the blast and then pretty well knocked senseless when the shattered carriage tumbled off the track and overturned. The explosion had lifted the carriage enough to uncouple it from the train, which meant that the guard's van and carriage with the strong room were also now left stranded on the plain, with the rest of the train steaming away into the distance.

The driver of the locomotive, who had been warned that some sort of attempt at robbery might be made that day, said to the engineer, 'What say, Jack? I stop or carry on?'

'Why, you damned fool, you speed up, of course. You want to get caught in the middle of a gun battle?'

The consequence was that the train, minus, of course, its last three coaches, continued on its way until it reached Claremont. From there, news of the robbery radiated outwards at the speed of light along the spider's web of telegraph wires which now covered that part of the United States. Within an hour of pulling into Claremont, lawmen all over Iowa and as far afield as Chicago had heard about the attempt to blow up the train carrying the silver from Carson City.

As the smoke cleared and it became apparent that the last few cars had been left behind, Seth Fraser gave a whoop of delight and said, 'Come on, boys, what you waiting for? Let's take that silver!' He rode off down the slope, with the other ten men strung out behind him.

The men from Claremont had hardly been in the saddle for five minutes before they heard an echoing boom which rolled across the open country like a clap of thunder. 'God almighty,' exclaimed Sheriff Palmer, 'what the hell was that?' He reined in and the men with him also halted. As they looked across the trees towards the direction from which the noise had come, they saw a column of smoke rising up into the sky. 'Shit,' said Palmer, 'unless I miss my guess, that's the bullion train. If you bastards had been a mite faster, we would a been there already. Ride, now. Ride like the wind!' He fitted his actions to his words and spurred his horse on; the others following his lead.

The carriage containing the silver was leaning at a crazy angle, half on the tracks and half off. The door at the end was hanging loose and open and it looked like all the Frasers and their men needed to do was climb right in and take their hundred thousand dollars. This at least was what Seth and Dan thought, except that as they began to dismount, somebody called from within the carriage, 'You bastards keep away. There are six of us in here and we are well armed.' This was something of

73

an exaggeration, although perhaps a pardonable one. There was only a clerk in there, in the barred compartment which held the silver coins. The money itself was in a huge safe, which occupied half the carriage.

Access to the bullion could only be gained by working the combination of the safe, which was large enough to walk inside and was really more like a strong room. The authorities were keenly aware of the possibility of collusion between employees and potential robbers and so had taken a special precaution. The clerk travelling with the train knew part of the combination and those at the journey's end in Chicago knew the other half. It was quite literally impossible to get into that safe unless you had the combination. It was built into the fabric of the carriage itself and was far too big to be removed. Because it was only moving about as part of a railway train, it could be as heavy as anybody cared to make it; which in this case meant quarter-inch steel plate all round, including the base. It would take a gallon of nitro-glycerin to break into that thing.

As soon as the clerk shouted his warning, the gang rode round to the other end of the carriage so that they were out of range of the windows. Dan Fraser, who was a notoriously vicious killer when the need arose, took his rifle from where it rested in a scabbard at the front of his saddle and said in a low voice, 'You all stay here. I will look into the matter.'

While the gang remained on their horses, waiting to see what would chance, Dan dismounted and crept along the side of the carriage, keeping low so that anybody looking from the windows would not be able to discern him. When he reached the doorway, where the door had been blown off its hinges, he cocked his rifle and then suddenly swung him-self up and marched straight inside. There were two shots in quick succession and then, just as everybody was wondering if he had been killed, Dan Fraser poked his head out from a window and growled,

'Are you lazy sons of bitches going to sit there playing with yourselves or do you want to come and fill your pockets with silver?'

As the posse came round the bend and saw the railroad line stretching before them, straight to the horizon, it was immediately apparent to them that a robbery was actually in progress. Even at that distance, they could see that a dozen horses were standing near three carriages and the riders were swarming over the wreckage like locusts. Sheriff Palmer called upon his men to halt. When they had done so, he said, 'Now listen up. Those thieving scoundrels have blown up a train. They will stick at naught. We are going to canter along now and then engage them in battle. I tell you straight, there will be a rich reward for taking them. The railroad company too will wish to show their gratitude. But let me tell you, I see any man hanging back now and trying to avoid danger and I will make sure that man does not see a cent of any reward money. Is that clear?'

It was clear, because the men riding in that posse had no other aim in the expedition beyond personal profit. They were fully prepared to risk their lives if the prize was high enough and from what Sheriff Palmer said, that was certainly the case here.

5

After Dan Fraser had killed the clerk in the carriage, the others quickly ran to collect their treasure. It was at this point that things began to go wrong in more ways than one. The safe was separated from the rest of the carriage by a wall of bars which stretched from ceiling to floor. The clerk was inside this cage-like arrangement and the gate leading in was locked. After some swearing and anger, somebody thought that maybe the clerk was carrying the key and had locked his own self into the cage. So it proved, because when they managed to drag his body over, a key on a chain which was attached to his belt was tried and this opened the gate and gave them access to the safe.

It did not take long to work out that there was not the slightest chance of them being able to open the strong room. Somebody was foolish enough to ask Seth Fraser if he had any more powder and if that might not do the trick? Seth grabbed this unfortunate fellow by his shirt front and slammed him against the wall. 'You stupid bastard,' he said, 'you think I carry kegs of powder around in my pants pockets? Look at that thing! It would take a sight more than ten pounds of powder to blast that open.'

Just as the realization was dawning upon them that they were stymied, one of those outside shouted a warning. 'There's riders coming down on us. I'd say it's a posse of some sort.'

There was a wild scramble to get to the horses and collect rifles. The horses were shepherded round to the opposite side of the carriage from that which the riders were approaching. Then they were tethered there and the men crouched alongside the carriage, sighting their rifles at the approaching body of men. Seth Fraser said, 'We'll all hang for this day's work if they catch us. You boys know that as well as I. So let's make sure that they don't catch us.'

There was not one of the men crouching and lying near that carriage who had not been carrying out a similar estimation of the state of affairs and if they were holding fire, it was only to ensure that the men coming towards them were close enough that they could be sure of killing them.

When they were somewhere in the region of sixty yards from the wrecked carriages, Sheriff Palmer reined in and his men did likewise. He called out, 'You men there. Throw down your weapons and I promise that you will stand a proper trial. There'll be no lynching or anything of that sort.' The words were no sooner out of his mouth than he fell off his horse dead, with a minie ball through his heart. Dan Fraser was a deadly shot and had no love at all for lawmen. As soon as he fired, the others in the gang also started shooting, pouring a withering fire into the riders. Before the startled men of the posse had a chance to respond, four more of them had been killed, in addition to the sheriff. One of these was the deputy and, left leaderless, the remaining three took flight.

There was not much rejoicing among the Frasers and their men, because the situation, as each man was only too well aware, was desperate. It was no longer a matter of not gaining ten thousand dollars worth of silver each; it was about whether or not they would hang. Had things gone according to plan and the train been stopped dead in its tracks, then it would have taken hours for news of the robbery to reach anybody. As it was, they all knew that by now the telegraph lines from Claremont would be buzzing and clacking and every town in the area would soon be alerted. A train robbery would have been bad enough, but now there was murder involved as well.

In the guard's van, there was one frightened employee of the railroad. He had been peeping fearfully through the window, watching the events unfold, as though he were at the theatre or something. After the massacre of the posse, he hunkered down and crouched in a corner, hoping and praying that the desperados would cut sticks and leave at once. He knew that his life wouldn't be worth a wooden dime if those men knew that there was a witness to their murders sitting a few yards from them.

There was another witness to the events that morning, but unlike the employee of the railroad, he was not a man who intended to take a passive role in such matters. Six of the Pinkerton's men had survived when Seth Fraser's mine exploded beneath them. Four of these were gravely injured; bleeding like stuck hogs, with limbs dangling uselessly. Two, though, were only shaken about and deafened by the blast. One of these men had no belly for further action, but the other was chilli-hot and thirsting for vengeance. He had not relinquished hold on his rifle when the bomb went off and now he crawled over to one of the firing ports and peered out. A bunch of men were standing around talking and he guessed that these were the cowardly assassins who had slaughtered his comrades. He cocked his piece, poked it from the slit and fired.

The swarthy fellow who Carnak suspected of having taken a dislike to him, was standing near to Dan Fraser, waiting to be told what the next move might entail. He was utterly devoted to the two brothers and would have given his life for them. This is more or less what he did, because the Pinkerton's man was drawing down on the two of them, wondering which would make the better target. In the end, he decided that the swarthy man was fatter and uglier than the thin man standing at his side. He aimed carefully at the man's face and squeezed the trigger of the Sharp's carbine.

Raoul, known to some as 'The greaser', was still looking anxiously at Dan Fraser's face, trying to divine what he ought to be doing. The ball took him in the cheek, below his left eye. It was deflected by his cheekbone into his nasal cavity, from where it drove up into his brain, killing him instantly.

None of the men in the gang had given any thought to the two carriages, which, along with the bullion van, had been left behind. Now, though, they reacted swiftly, some diving for cover and others racing towards the carriage from where the shot had come. The first man to reach the carriage saw that it had a door, which he at once tried. It was locked. He drew his pistol and then slid noiselessly along the side of the carriage, until he was beneath the rifle barrel which was protruding from a slit in the side of the van. He jumped up, grabbing the rifle barrel as he did so. Then he at once emptied his pistol into the interior of the carriage, hearing with satisfaction a cry of pain. He pulled the rifle out and threw it to one side. Another man came running up, his rifle in his hand. He looked into the carriage, his eyes taking a few moments to become accustomed to the darkness within. Then, when he had identified a groaning man, he shot him. There looked to be other men in there and so he drew his pistol and shot them as well.

'You men,' said Dan Fraser, 'check that other van. Kill anybody you find.'

They needed no second bidding and three of them went to the guard's van and opened the door. The occupant, a balding, middle-aged man, was crouched in a corner whimpering. 'Don't hurt me!' he mumbled meaninglessly, before he was silenced forever by a perfect fusillade of fire.

Once they had killed everybody in sight who did not belong to their own party, including the surviving witnesses in the Pinkertons' coach, the Frasers wasted no time in setting everybody on the right path. Seth said, 'That train will be in Claremont by now and an hour later, they will be raising posses from here to Chicago. We must get back to our homes. But mark what I say. We are not going to race for home all together, not by a long chalk. Any tracker worth his salt would follow the marks of ten horses riding together as plain as plain.'

'What do you advise?' asked somebody.

'Advise?' asked Seth Fraser in surprise. 'Advise? I ain't about to advise you. I am telling you what you will all do, which is this. We break into three groups. Me, Dan, you, Casey and you, Carnak, will ride together. You three over there, yes you, will be another party and the rest will make up a third. Don't be coming into Jacksonville from the north, because it will be a dead giveaway. They too will have heard news of this by the time we arrive.'

'What then?' somebody asked.

'Go round it in a long curve and come in from the south. It will mean us all sleeping out tonight, but that's nothing. Better a night out in the open than being hanged. You three, get saddled up now and on your way. Head east for ten miles, maybe, and then change direction and make for south of Jacksonville.'

Once the three men had left, the others made some slight provision for their dead friend, scraping a shallow grave for him and piling rocks over the corpse. Before doing this, they removed identifying marks from his shirt, where he had written his name in it.

Nobody felt like complaining to the Frasers about being put in hazard of their very lives in this way and for no profit at all. Most of the time, the Frasers were on the mark and if once in a while things miscarried, well that was life. Nobody was forced to ride with them.

After the second group left, the Frasers saddled up and told Carnak and Casey to do likewise. Then they headed west for a space, intending to cut round south after a few hours.

★　★　★

There was consternation at the Pinkertons' head office when the news came in of the abortive raid on the train. Nobody knew any details yet, other than that the train that Pinkertons had been guarding had been damaged by an explosion and the silver was missing. That such an affair could take place within two hundred miles of the Pinkertons' headquarters! It was very bad publicity. It was one thing for games of this kind to be perpetrated out West somewhere; but only a relatively short distance from one of the most prosperous and civilized cities in the United States? It was unthinkable and showed Pinkertons in a very poor light. Alan Pinkerton was determined to find out what had happened. Then he wanted to track down and kill those responsible for the debacle. There was no news at that stage of what had actually befallen his men.

Before taking any action, Pinkerton thought that the first step should be to find just what that man Mitford had been up to. He accordingly went with a couple of assistants down to Mitford's office to see what details he could uncover there. The answer to that was: precious few. Everything should have been in Mitford's safe, but there was nothing at all about the case there bar some background information on the Frasers and the suspicions which were attached to them.

'Ach, there must be something written down,' fumed the old man. 'Dinna tell me ye can't find it.'

The two men going through the contents of Mitford's safe shook their heads dubiously. It was not at all uncommon for men like Mitford, working on a big case, to keep everything in their heads. The only thing that Alan Pinkerton cared about was success and if a man like Mitford pulled off a coup like capturing the Frasers, then the old man would be unlikely to fuss about the paucity of records.

'We can ask round the other

departments, sir,' suggested one of his personal assistants, 'if that would help?'

Pinkerton tended when angry to revert to the coarser and more direct modes of speech from his youth. He did so now, roaring, 'For the love of God, just pull your finger out of your arse and get me some results. Ye're no more use than a lassie.'

* * *

When Dale Carnak rode off with the Fraser brothers and the other man, whom he had hardly exchanged more than a word or two with, he began to try to think like a lawman. If he was indeed working for Pinkertons, then what should he be doing now? The main thing was that he knew for sure that the Frasers were leading this gang and that this could lead to many robberies being cleared up and solved. This was a good beginning, but it didn't tell him what his next course of action should be. He supposed that there was no tearing hurry, because once they were back in Jacksonville, he would be able to wire Pinkertons and tell them what he had discovered.

Now what Carnak did not know was that his neck was in greater peril than that of any of the real members of the Fraser brothers' gang. This was because of a mix-up at the Pinkertons' office in Chicago.

It sometimes happened that men working at the headquarters in Chicago would get the printers to turn out a wanted bill or something like that featuring one of their friends or even a fellow worker. These 'spoof' items caused a good deal of amusement. One day, somebody had even turned out a wanted poster featuring Alan Pinkerton himself, with various distinguishing characteristics such as, 'Unable to speak like a normal citizen' and 'Swears like a trooper'. When Chris Mitford wanted to create a 'legend' for Carnak, he had taken his details down to the printers and asked for them to be included in a special 'one-off' leaflet which he would send off to Jacksonville himself.

The best laid plans can miscarry and that is just precisely what happened in the case of the leaflet which Mitford had arranged to send to Jacksonville. Because once he had the finished article, he did not trouble himself about the draft which he had handed to the printer. As a result, when this man had finished for the day, Mitford's description of Dale Carnak had somehow or other got mixed up with some genuine paperwork and as a result, almost every lawman in the northern part of the state of Iowa was advised to look out for him, having been told that he was suspected of being involved in holding up a train in Kansas.

When the three men from the posse which had set out from Claremont returned to town, the news that they bore was greeted with first incredulity and then fierce anger. Sheriff Palmer had been well liked in the town and that he had been murdered while doing his duty was shocking news. Just like Alan Pinkerton, the citizens of Claremont had thought that they were near enough to civilized parts not to be at risk of real violence of this sort. That evening, a meeting took place at the biggest saloon in the town. Sheriff Palmer might be dead, but there were a number of men who thought they knew what to do next, which was to get after the murdering sons of bitches who had killed their sheriff and then string them up from the nearest tree.

The lights were burning late in the Pinkertons' headquarters that night. Pinkertons had many informants in regular law enforcement agencies and by evening, the news had come through via Claremont that when a posse had arrived at the scene of the robbery, there was no sign of anybody alive apart from those who had seemingly carried out the attack. It was beginning to look as though every member of the group headed by Mitford was missing.

'What was laddie boy Mitford up to?' asked Pinkerton of a man who had been working under him. 'I asked him straight, d'ye have a man on the inside? 'No,' he told me. I canna fathom it out, ye ken?'

The man coughed discreetly. It was being rumoured round the building that Chris Mitford was almost certainly dead and, that being the case, a man had to think of his own interests.

'What are ye coughin' for, man? Are ye ill? Or d'ye have something to tell me? If so, then out with it.'

'It's like this, sir,' said the man hesitantly, 'I don't like to be telling tales, if you take my meaning, but — '

At this point, Alan Pinkerton cut in with the greatest irascibility, saying, 'Time's precious, man. If ye're knowing anything about this, why then, ye better tell me this minute.'

'There was somebody on the inside, sir. A fellow called Carnak.'

'How d'ye know? Was Mitford after tellin' ye?'

'Not exactly, no sir. Here's the way of it. You might know that sometimes the men have spoof bills and suchlike printed?'

'Spoof? What are ye talkin' of?'

The fellow explained about the spoof printing which was sometimes undertaken. He went on, 'Mr Mitford wanted a special version of one of our leaflets done, with this man, Dale Carnak's name and description in it. I heard about it from the fellow in the printing shop.'

'I mind there's been some high jinks going on here,' said Pinkerton in his rich brogue, sounding like a disapproving Scottish minister who has just learned of some disgraceful goings on, 'Some of you men seem to think ye're working the music halls or something of the sort, the way ye've been carrying on. Can you find me a copy of this description?'

They found one of the leaflets after some rooting around in the print shop. Pinkerton asked,

'So ye're sayin' that this fellow, yon Carnak, was engaged to work in with the Fraser gang?'

'That's what it looks like, sir, yes.'

* * *

The Frasers and the other two men rode hard for some hours after the raid on the train. Dusk overtook them about twelve miles southwest of Jacksonville. The Frasers said that it would be a good idea to rest up and then return to their homes the following day. The sight of men riding through the night would be sure to invite questions, especially with the alarm likely to have been raised by the train robbery. The four of them found a little clearing in the woods, not far from a tiny hamlet and there they built a fire and brewed up some coffee. They had the remains of their breakfast to dine off and pretty slim pickings it made too. Under other circumstances, it might have been possible to steal a chicken or something from a farm, but with the countryside roused by their actions, this would have been too likely to draw attention to them.

When they had eaten what they had and finished off the coffee, Seth Fraser seemed disposed to talk. The failure of the train robbery was not a disaster for him and his brother; it was more in the nature of an annoyance. One way or another, he and his brother had enough squirrelled away to tide them over for a good long spell and unlike most of those who rode with them, the Fraser spread did actually make money. They were outlaws more by inclination than necessity. They always liked to have more money than they already had and also enjoyed the act of robbery and murder.

'So tell me about this train that you knocked over in Kansas.' said Seth to Dale Carnak.

Now until that moment, it had never occurred to Carnak that he would be put in a position where he had to maintain the imposture of being a dangerous outlaw to other people's faces. It was one thing to have a wanted poster circulated; another to discuss the details of armed robbery with men who were experts on the subject.

'Never said anything about robbing no train,' said Carnak gruffly. 'Don't recollect claiming any such thing.'

'Ah come on,' said Seth, 'You're among friends here. How did you go about it?'

Dale Carnak was not really in the habit of lying and deceiving others. Howsoever, on this occasion, his very life could be cast into hazard if he did not make a good fist of it and so he felt that he at least needed to make the attempt. He recalled what one of the Frasers had said about red lanterns and decided to use that for the starting point.

'Here's the way of it,' said Carnak, horribly aware that his life could depend upon the story he was about to tell and hoping that he would not blush or stammer, as he was prone to do when telling lies, 'There were seven of us. You know the AT and SF line that runs into Topeka?'

'Sure,' said Seth, 'know it well, don't we, Dan? We did a little business down that way ourselves once.'

'Well, there's a branch runs up to a place called Buffalo Springs. It ain't nothing special — little town. We took it into our heads to wait for the train to pass from there, heading down into Topeka.'

'Was it carrying anything much?' asked Dan Fraser, his professional interest aroused.

'No, we just went after the passengers. We swung a red lantern on the line ahead of it, just where it was due to run down to the main AT and SF. Well, it stopped and then we tied up the driver and engineer and just set to on those passengers.'

'You get much?' asked Casey.

'Not really. Just wallets and watches, really. But it beat working for a living.'

There were guffaws of laughter as Carnak concluded his account and he was pleasantly surprised to find that he could, when need be, spin a yarn as well as any, more practiced, liar.

6

The morning of Wednesday, 13 April began early for the staff at the Pinkertons head office, with the old man rampaging around the place raising hell. By nine, it had been learned from several sources that all the agents who had been travelling on that train were dead. This was in addition to the railroad guard and the five members of the posse. The massacre of twenty people was the worst crime anybody could remember since the end of the war.

To be fair to Alan Pinkerton, he was genuinely grieved about the deaths of so many of his men and declared that he would take care of their families and that their sacrifice would not be forgotten. He had a more practical grudge, though, against the men who had committed such a dreadful crime and that was that it made his organization look mighty foolish. It was one thing for such shenanigans to take place out in the wild frontier country, but for it to happen a bare two hundred miles from his own headquarters did not reflect at all well on the Pinkertons Detective Agency. Pinkertons had guaranteed the safety of that train; how could people trust his firm again?

There was an obvious explanation for the failure of his men to protect the train and it was one that tied in with certain suspicions that were currently floating round the agency. These were to the effect that there were traitors at work in Pinkertons; criminals who had wormed their way into the agency solely to pass on information to their villainous associates on the outside.

The attack on the train from Carson City was not the only recent operation that had been compromised in this way and Alan Pinkerton was determined to get to the bottom of the matter. Fact is, he had already more than half made up his mind where the blame lay. That morning at half past nine, he called a special meeting of the seven heads of departments and laid out his thoughts to them.

'Seems to me,' he said, 'that things have been getting vairy, vairy slack in this place. The print room has been abused for jokes, staff taken on all over the shop, without so much as a by-your-leave. Well, I can tell you men, it's all going to stop now, d'ye ken?'

The seven men nodded their heads and did their best to look shocked and horrified at what the old man was telling them.

'My gut tells me,' continued Pinkerton, 'that this operation, guarding the train, was betrayed. Yes, I say betrayed. Somebody took our money and then set up those men to be slain without mercy.'

Nobody said anything, which appeared to irritate Alan Pinkerton, because he said, 'Och, what ails you all? Ye sit there like two pennorth a Gawd help us, without a thought in your heads. What am I paying you for?'

'Who do you think betrayed us, sir?' ventured one of the departmental heads at length.

'If it isn't as plain as the nose on your face,' said Pinkerton, 'it was young fella-me-lad that Mitford engaged. This Dale Carnak. He took the money that was given him, hooked up with those bandits and then double crossed us by joining the gang and selling our men to them.'

This theory certainly had its attractions. For one thing, if an outsider was to blame, then that let them off the hook entirely. If the old man's attention was altogether focused upon this Carnak, then he might forget to make inquiries about who else on his staff had been having spoof wanted bills printed or paying out money to mythical informers to supplement their official salaries.

'What should we do about it, sir?' asked somebody. 'Do you want us to pass on our suspicions to the regular law enforcement agencies?'

'I see we've already sent out this man's description,' observed Pinkerton, 'as part of some long game that Chris Mitford was playing. Now it's nay just ourselves alone as has suffered from this. There's men in a posse been gunned down and also some poor chap from the railroad. I want a 'special' to leave this city in four hours at most. I want at least a dozen of our best men on it and they can take their mounts with them. It can stop at Claremont. While ye're arranging that, somebody find a good, big map of Jacksonville, Claremont and all round there. Let's see if we can run these foxes to earth.'

* * *

Two events took place in Iowa at about the time that Alan Pinkerton was berating his men, both of which had a bearing on the case that he was hoping to solve. The first thing happened in the open country between Claremont and Jacksonville.

The three men who set off first from the scene of the failed train robbery were all sodbusters from farms around Jacksonville. Their names were Jake Carter, Abednego Williams and Tom Wright. All three of them were in their twenties and just about scraped enough of a living from their smallholdings to feed their wives and children. That was about all they did manage from the produce of their fields and when it came to new clothes or anything of that kind, they were often at a loss. Tom Wright's 8-year-old daughter wore an old flour sack in the main about the fields and the other men's families were not in much better case.

Riding with the Frasers made the difference for these men between struggling to survive and being just one step ahead of starvation on the one hand and being able to buy new shoes for the little ones and set meat on the table regularly, on the other. They were none of them outlaws by inclination, but when the Devil drives behind you,

you never know where you will wind up.

Despite all the warnings given them by Seth and Dan Fraser, as soon as they were out of sight of the brothers, the men did not take over-seriously the danger that they faced. They had been in fixes before, maybe not as bad as this one, but had always managed to make it home and live to ride another day. They were all three of them men of little imagination and simply did not conceive the anger which their massacre of the posse had caused in the town from which it came.

Carter, Williams and Wright made little or no efforts at concealment when they camped up that night. Their wide sweep east, intending to bring them down towards Jacksonville, had taken them closer to Claremont than was wise. The meeting in the saloon in that town on the evening of the 12th had, in the absence of Sheriff Palmer to act as a moderating influence, turned into something so close to being a lynch mob as made no odds. There was no question of the men, half of whom were liquored up anyway, going home and sleeping on matters. Instead, they saddled up at about eleven that night and rode out looking at once for whoever they could find that might have had a hand in the murders.

Abednego Williams was the first of the trio to awaken on the morning following the ambush of the train from Carson City. He poked up the embers of the fire and then added a few twigs and leaves to get it going. Then he went over to a lone tree, in the lee of which he and his two companions had spent the night, reached up and twisted off a few green branches to see if they would burn. It was still only the middle of April and the mornings were a mite chilly that far north.

Williams' only aim was to get a little blaze going to warm himself and he could not in a hundred years have guessed that he was signing not only his own death warrant, but also those of the two men who were still sleeping.

The green wood snapped and hissed, giving off clouds of fragrant smoke, which trickled up into the clear morning sky. Two miles away, the men who had set out from Claremont the night before were feeling dog-tired and weary enough to fall asleep in the saddle. They had quartered the land surrounding Claremont without catching hide nor hair of the men they were looking for. Another half hour and they probably would have been turning to home. Then one of the men said, 'Look over yonder. What do you make to that smoke?'

'Well, there ain't no farm in that direction and that's a fact,' replied the man next to him, 'and it's a strange time of year to be out hunting. You want we should take a look-see?'

'What do you say, boys?' said one of the others. 'Ride over and see what's to do and then if it's nothing, go home and start looking again this afternoon?' There were grunts of assent and eleven heavily armed riders went cantering across the plain towards the curl of smoke.

'Hey, wake up you fellows!' said Williams, prodding his partners with his toe. 'Time to make tracks.'

The other two men stirred and then cursed Abednego roundly as they came to. 'What the hell did you wake us for?' said Tom Wright. 'What's the hurry?'

'We gotta get out of this neighbourhood,' said Williams, 'lest . . . hark, what's that? Can you hear hoofs?'

They all listened carefully, but by the time they were sure that a body of horsemen was riding down on them at speed, it was a little late to be doing anything about it. A few seconds later, they all saw the riders, silhouetted on a ridge some half a mile away. Jake Carter snatched up his rifle, but Williams snarled at him to set it down again. 'You damned fool,' he said, 'can't you see there's at least a dozen of them? We start a shooting match and whatever harm we do them, we'll all of us be killed. Let's bluff it out.'

The grim-faced men who trotted down the slope and surrounded them did not look to be in the best of moods for parlaying and long conversation. The effects of the intoxicating liquor of which they had been imbibing the night before had all worn off and they had not slept. All of them looked right irritable and short tempered and Abednego Williams wondered too late if he had not made a mistake in advising his friends not to pick up their weapons. There were worse things than being shot.

Two of the riders dismounted and collected up their guns while the other nine men covered them with their rifles and scatterguns. Williams tried to put on a gruff and outraged voice, but so afeared was he, that it came out as high and querulous. 'What in the hell are you men doing? What gives you the right to take our stuff? You bushwhackers or something of that sort?'

It was a valiant attempt, but doomed to failure. One of the men who had been collecting their rifles and pistols began sniffing at the barrels. He did this with every weapon and then told the other men, 'They've been fired recent. All of them.'

One of the unsmiling men looking down on them said, 'We are looking for some men who killed a friend of us. Killed him and a bunch of others. You look to fit the bill. Where you been and where you going?'

Tom Wright said, 'We been hunting last night. Camped out.'

'Hunting? What you been hunting with pistols and rifles both?'

There was no answer. The man said, 'You tell us the truth and maybe we will just take you into town and let the law deal with you.'

Carter, the youngest of the three, thought this sounded like a chance of escaping summary justice out here in the wild and said, 'We didn't kill your friends, it was others as was with us.'

'Shut up, you cowson,' said Williams, appalled. 'You given them the excuse they need to kill us right now.'

'You said you'd take us for a fair trial, didn't you, mister?' said Jake Carter. 'Said you'd take us in to the law and all?'

'I lied,' said the man. He called over to another of the riders, 'Joe, you got your Bible with you?'

'You know I never go anywhere without the word of the Lord tucked right there in my saddle-bag,' said an older, white-haired man. 'Why, you want it?'

'Yes,' said the fellow who seemed to be the nearest thing to a leader that this band had. 'Fetch it over, please. You don't mind me lending it to somebody?'

'Why no, I'm always glad to see unbelievers read scripture.'

When the old man who had been addressed as Joe rode up, the other man directed him to hand the small black volume to Williams, who looked at it in bewilderment. 'What's the idea?' he asked.

'In half an hour, you hang. You and these other two. You might want to say a few prayers or something of the sort before you die.'

'No, you can't,' said Jake Carter. 'You promised. You can't just hang us. You know it wouldn't be right.'

'Save your breath,' advised the man who had pronounced their doom. 'You will soon have need of it.'

When the time came to hang the three men, Williams and Wright met their deaths stoically enough. It took three men, though, to drag Jake Carter to the waiting noose, with the young man screaming and struggling all the way. He died hard as well, kicking convulsively for almost five minutes after he had been suspended from the tree branch.

* * *

Dale Carnak woke very early on the Wednesday morning and found that the thoughts that he had been working on over the last few weeks had crystalized, until they were set as firm as iron. He had no further doubt that he had actually been engaged as a lawman by the Pinkertons Detective Agency and he was aiming to act accordingly. The murders that he had witnessed had been pretty bad, but then again he had seen worse than that during the war. No, what had decided him was that he had been offered a job of work and he was going to complete it. He hadn't made a whole lot of his life since the war ended, but here was a chance to change all that and build a proper, respectable career for himself; something which he had not essayed before in his short life.

The sun had barely risen above the horizon when Carnak was already up and doing. While Casey and the Frasers slumbered, he gathered up all their weapons and emptied them of powder and shot and cartridges. Then he threw them into the nearby bushes so they were out of sight.

Carnak checked that his rifle was cocked and his pistol nice and loose in its holster. Then he prodded Casey awake with the barrel of the rifle. 'Hey,' he said, 'bestir yourself. There's something I would tell you.'

'What the hell is it, Carnak?' said the sleepy man. 'Lord God, but it's early.'

'Here's how the case stands,' said Carnak, 'I am working for the Pinkertons Detective Agency and you three men are all my prisoners.'

Casey laughed, his irritation fading. 'Jesus, Carnak, you are a joker and no mistake. Wait till I tell Seth what you said. He will bust himself laughing.'

'Why don't you rouse him and tell him?' suggested Carnak, his face stony. 'I dare say he could do with a laugh.'

'Shit, you're not joshing, are you?'

'Not hardly. Wake up those two.'

Casey shook Seth and Dan Fraser awake, while Carnak stood well back, covering them all with his rifle. The Fraser brothers were not best pleased to be shaken awake so roughly and they cursed Casey and his mother in the coarsest terms. Then they spotted Dale Carnak standing there with his gun pointing at them. Seth said, 'What's the case, young Carnak?'

'Here it is. I am working for Pinkertons and all you three are wanted for murder. I aim to take you into Jacksonville and hand you over to the law.'

'If this is a joke . . . ' began Seth Fraser, reaching surreptitiously for his pistol. When he realized that it was not where he had left it, he began scrabbling round for his rifle instead. He could not lay his hands on that either and it was then that it dawned on him that the young man he had himself recruited into the gang was in deadly earnest. A Pinkerton's man!

Dan Fraser stared at the man holding him at gunpoint. He hated all lawmen, but reserved a special loathing and detestation for Pinkertons, who he regarded as little better than mercenaries. At least the sheriffs and marshals were working for the public good, even if their ideas didn't exactly coincide with his own view of things. But the Pinkertons just hunted men down for money, like bounty killers. Dan Fraser said in a low voice, 'You are as good as dead, Carnak, you know that?'

'We'll see,' replied Carnak, cheerfully enough, 'Now you all get dressed and saddle up. I will shoot at the least excuse and if I miss one of you, you may be certain-sure that I will hit the others.'

There being little other choice, the three men sullenly pulled on their boots and prepared to move out, with Carnak covering them the whole while. As he had intimated, even if one of them was not in range, if trouble started, then he would be sure to kill at least one or two others. Under the circumstances, there was little for them to do but follow his instructions.

7

In Chicago, Alan Pinkerton had had a large map of Jacksonville and the surrounding area pinned up on a board and set at the front of a spare room. Some of his best men were sitting there now, facing the front of the room, while Pinkerton himself stood by the map and pointed out various features that occurred to him. It looked for all the world like a geography lesson taking place in a schoolroom.

'Ye ken, here's where the train was jumped. And now here's Jacksonville, where those precious Fraser brothers and their boys hang out. Well now, here's the play. Ye've blown up the train and killed a bunch of folk. Now ye're wanting to run back home. What would ye be doing?'

From the back of the room, a man said, 'I wouldn't go straight there, that's for sure. I reckon that now word is out about this business, there might be men from Jacksonville out looking for the robbers, too. Anybody coming from the direction of the railroad line will be suspicioned at once.'

The old man beamed as though a favourite pupil had completed a recitation perfectly. 'Aye, there's brains for ye. That's the way of it, without a doubt. Why the Devil canna ye all think like that?'

Pinkerton pulled out a thick pencil and scribbled a large black spot on the map of Jacksonville, a little to the south. 'Now whist,' he said, 'this is where the Frasers live with their mama. They will be hoping to tiptoe back home and then make out they've been safely tucked up in bed all the time during this crime. Well, you men are to put them straight on that score. I have engaged a special to take you all down to Claremont this very day. Ye'll be there by evening.'

One or two of the men exchanged meaningful glances. The railroad sometimes let privately chartered trains use their lines, which were given precedence over regular, scheduled services. It was fantastically expensive to hire the use of a main line in this fashion and they knew that Alan Pinkerton very seldom took such a step. That he was prepared to throw money around to this extent now was a measure of how much importance he attached to this case. This was an added incentive for the agents assembled in the room not to make a hash of the enterprise. Whoever broke up the gang that had ambushed the train and killed fourteen Pinkerton's men would be in the old man's good books for a good long while to come.

While this debate was taking place two hundred miles away, Dale Carnak and his three prisoners were making their way slowly towards Jacksonville. He rode at the back, with the Frasers in front of him and Jim Casey in front of them. Carnak felt instinctively that the Fraser brothers would willingly sacrifice Casey and so he wanted to be sure that he had them covered and that they were both well aware that if he started shooting, it was them that would be stopping bullets in their backs, rather than somebody else.

Carnak did not trust the Frasers an inch and was under no illusions at all about the fact that they would most likely make a bolt for it before they reached town. That was up to them. For his part, he had behaved correctly and if they wished to gamble their lives in that way, there was little that he could do to prevent them.

Seth called back to him in a friendly fashion, saying, 'You are awful young to be a Pinkerton's man. Would you like to tell us how that came to pass?'

'I would not,' said Carnak firmly. 'It is enough for you to know that I am working for Pinkertons and that I am handing you over to the law in Jacksonville.'

'Don't talk to the little bastard,' said Dan Fraser peevishly, 'he's a skunk. Who knows what will befall him between here and Jacksonville?'

The sheriff in Jacksonville had heard by now about the attack on the train from Carson City and he, like other lawmen, hoped that it would be his good fortune to apprehend the bandits. To that end, he had raised two bands of men who were prowling the countryside, looking for any members of the gang. Nobody had the least idea that it was men from round there who had been responsible for such an atrocious crime.

The posse led by the Jacksonville sheriff, a decent man by the name of Orville Larssen, had been spiralling out from the town for the last few hours, circling carefully on the off chance that they would come across some of the outlaws who had carried out the massacre. They almost bumped right into Dale Carnak and his captives and at first, he was mightily relieved to see them.

Sheriff Larssen and the seven men in his group were eight or ten miles from town, heading east along a little track, when they saw three local men being held up at gunpoint. That at least was how the situation presented itself to them and their belief that this was what was happening was strengthened when the Fraser brothers caught sight of the posse and began waving and shouting for help.

When the eight men came close, Sheriff Larssen shouted for Carnak to throw down his weapon. To emphasize that he was not fooling, every member of his party of riders drew down on Carnak and it was very clear that if he did not comply, then he would not live a great dealer longer. He threw down the rifle. He was then further advised to toss the pistol from his belt, moving very slowly as he did so. This too, he did.

'Orville,' said Seth Fraser, 'thank God we saw you. This young rascal got the drop on us and was planning to do the Lord knows what. If you hadn't come along, God only knows what he would have done.'

Sheriff Larssen was no sort of fool. For all that he knew the Fraser brothers right well, he had never managed to figure out how that farm of theirs kept them in quite such means as they displayed when in town. There was also something a little strange about this claim that Seth and his brother had been jumped by this young fellow. Larssen had a good memory for faces and kept a close watch on what went on in Jacksonville. He was pretty sure that he had seen Seth walking the streets in the company of this very man that he was now representing to be a stranger. Something didn't add up.

'What's your name, son?' Sheriff Larssen asked Carnak, who told him at once.

'You're Dale Carnak? You know that your name is all over the state and beyond as a man involved in a massacre up at the railroad? What do you say to that?'

'I say I'm working for the Pinkertons Detective Agency and these three men are the ones you want for that job.'

Sheriff Larssen had an extra cat's sense when it came to criminals. Notwithstanding that this fellow's name was circulating on the wires as being a likely suspect in the affair, he could not square it with his own feelings as he looked into the young man's face. His deputy had also found the leaflet that Pinkertons had sent them a couple of weeks ago and remarked to Larssen that it did not surprise him to hear about this here Dale Carnak, because they had already been warned about him; all the evidence pointed towards Carnak, the man before him now. Even so, Larssen hesitated.

While Larssen was figuring all this out, Seth Fraser interrupted his thoughts, saying, 'Orville, you have known me and my brother these twenty years. We are upstanding citizens of Jacksonville and I am grieved that you seem to be doubtful of your duty.'

Dan thought his brother was overdoing the outraged citizen act a little and wished that Seth would just shut up. Sheriff Larssen said, 'I don't need you or any man to teach me my job, Seth. Things don't total up right here and that is the fact of the matter.' He turned to Carnak and said, 'You may be telling the truth and then again you may not. We will look into this closely when we get back to town. In the meantime, I am going to have to handcuff you. My deputy will move up to you and do so, but mind that there are another six men with their pieces cocked and just waiting to fire on you. Don't be a fool.'

While the deputy was snapping the steel cuffs on Carnak, Larssen was still thinking that something wasn't right about this whole setup. Seth Fraser was still saying nothing about knowing this Carnak and that in itself was strange. Why was he so keen to have him, Orville Larssen, think that they were strangers to each other?

'Seth,' said the sheriff, 'and you too, Dan and you, Casey, you had best come along with us now to town. This all bears looking into deeply and I don't intend to conduct my inquiries setting here in the road.'

Both Seth and Dan were wishing that these men would just string up Carnak on the spot and thus prevent a heap of embarrassing questions being asked. Already, Seth was kicking himself for giving the sheriff the impression that this was some stranger they had just met on the road. How would that be so if Larssen had seen them in each other's company when Carnak was staying in town?

This tricky situation for the Frasers was solved in the neatest way imaginable. Dale Carnak was starting to panic about being taken back to Jacksonville. He had read lurid accounts in the newspapers about the vigilantes dragging the members of the Reno gang out of New Albany gaol and hanging them in the town square. He had no illusions about such things and had a feeling that if once he was lodged in the sheriff's office in Jacksonville, the Frasers might incite the folk in the town to behave in a similar way towards him.

Not for nothing had Carnak been known in the 3rd Kentucky Horse as the smartest young rider in the outfit. During the war, if ever they wanted a message conveyed across difficult or hostile terrain, it was always for Carnak that somebody would send. He had an uncanny ability for negotiating tricky land and dodging bullets. The men of the Jacksonville posse, sitting at ease upon their mounts, could have had no idea about this. All they saw was a dejected and disarmed young man with his wrists cuffed securely in front of him.

With not the slightest indication of what he was about to do, Carnak spurred his horse on, jabbing it viciously in the flanks. The creature leapt forward like a scalded cat, pushing between two riders that stood in its path; so close that the men could have reached out and shaken Dale Carnak's hand as he passed, had they been quick enough. Then the young man was galloping hell for leather across level country towards a line of trees a few hundred yards away.

Now when some horseman is racing away from you at top speed in this fashion, you only have two options open to you and these are to open fire or ride off in pursuit. A few of the men fired at the fleeing rider, but already he was far enough not to make it likely that he would be brought down by rifle fire. Sheriff Larssen cursed and then shouted at his men to give chase. Some of them pulled their pistols as they did so and fired wildly at Carnak, who was already over a hundred yards ahead of them and nearing the trees. This was purely a waste of powder and shot, though, because no man can aim with any sort of accuracy while perched on a galloping horse.

Their quarry entered the wood and those in pursuit spurred on their horses, feeling exceedingly foolish not to have anticipated an escape of this sort.

Dale Carnak was jinking to and fro,

dodging tree roots and so on, with no real notion of how successful this was likely to be. Behind him, he heard shouts that told him that he had been spotted through the trees and he peered desperately ahead to see if there was any hope of open country again. From experience, he guessed that those chasing after him would now be spreading out in a line, so that they could outflank him, should he take it into his head to try to double back on his tracks and evade them in that way.

The posse was gaining on him, but more by luck than judgment. He was taking care to dodge every obstacle and slowing from time to time to avoid his horse breaking a leg in a rabbit hole. Those chasing him were more careless of their horses' welfare and were pressing on fast. It was a miracle none of them took a fall, but there it was.

Thankfully, the trees were becoming more and more sparse and Carnak found himself back in open country, which favoured his escape. He rode forward and then noticed something which gave him hope that he really might make it. The flat land ahead was cut by a river, which over the years had carved a miniature canyon across the landscape. It was not a mighty river, being no more than ten feet or so in width, but the valley it had dug had steeply sloping sides, with little chance of a horse being able to find its way down to the water or up again the other side. The drop from the level land down to the water was only fifteen foot or so, but the important distance was that from side to side.

As he bore down on the river, Carnak tried to gauge the jump that would be needed to get clear from one side of the little ravine to the other. It looked to him to be at least twenty feet, which was one hell of a jump. Still and all, he had very little choice. When a man has the fear of death at his back, he is apt to take greater risks than is usually the case.

Carnak looked back and saw that the

pursuers were also clear of the trees and were only a hundred yards behind him. He slowed for a second and patted his horse affectionately and then spurred her on again as hard as he could. She shot forward and then he was approaching the jump at a gallop. At the last moment, his nerve almost failed him and he was sure that both he and the horse would end up falling short and crashing into the almost vertical side of the little canyon, across the river. It was too late to stop, though, and just as they reached the edge of the drop, he gave his horse a sharp dig and threw himself forward in the saddle for extra impetus.

The horse sailed up into the air and across the river. It seemed to Carnak that they were suspended for a time in mid-air, with the river beneath him and the sound of the riders thundering from behind. Then they were across, with barely six inches to spare behind his horse's hind hoofs as they landed. It had been the closest of shaves.

There was no time to congratulate

himself on his horsemanship and Carnak set off again at a gallop, wondering if any of those after him would dare to make the same jump.

All eight men slowed down as they reached the river. They knew this area and not one of them had ever heard tell of a rider jumping the thing this far down stream. They gazed in impotent wrath at the fast vanishing figure of the rider who was now beyond their reach. Nobody even had the heart to send a few shots after him; the range was too great.

'That's one hell of a rider,' said Sheriff Larssen. 'I never heard of anybody jumping the river here. It's over twenty foot from side to side.'

'You sound like you admire him, Sheriff,' said one of the other men. 'Recollect what the murdering son of a bitch done.'

'Don't know what he's done,' said Larssen evenly. 'Ain't yet had a chance to ask him.'

'Speaks for itself, don't it?' said

another man. 'He dug up and ran. If that's not a sign of guilt, why then I don't know what is!'

'Maybe,' said Sheriff Larssen. 'Come on, let's get back and see what those Frasers have got to say about all this.'

The Frasers had been pleased and relieved when Dale Carnak cut sticks in that way. There was no telling what foolishness he would have come out with had he stayed around. As soon as the posse had gone off in pursuit, Dan had said to Casey, 'You get off to your home now. And just keep your damned mouth shut about all this, unless you want to hang.'

Casey hadn't needed to be told twice and left without another word. He had privately decided that he would never again ride with the Fraser brothers. The last few days had taken him from the farm and he had nothing to show for his absence, other than the shadow of the gallows. The game was no longer worth the candle, as far as he could see.

After Casey had left them, the

Frasers smoked for a while and then Seth said, 'I reckon that's us home and dry. Either they'll kill that fellow or he'll get away. There's nothing to link us to that train.'

'Meaning we killed all the witnesses,' said his brother. 'Yes, that was a right smart move.'

'What about those of that posse that surprised us there?' said Seth. 'You think they could identify us?'

'No, they never got close enough. I reckon we're clear.'

When Larssen and his posse returned, it was without their erstwhile prisoner, which gave a lift to the spirits of the Fraser brothers. The sheriff's eyes narrowed as he saw Seth and Dan chatting casually and laughing at some private joke. He knew in his bones that there was more going on here than met the eye.

Seth said, 'Well, Orville, me and my brother here are much obliged to you for rescuing us. There's no telling what would have been our fate had you and your boys not come along. What a mercy that was!'

Sheriff Larssen looked at Seth and replied coolly, 'There is more investigation needful in this matter, Seth. I hope you and your brother are not going to be travelling out of the district in a hurry?'

'Us?' said Seth, innocently, 'No, Orville. We will be right there on our farm, working away all the hours God sends, just as usual. You come by any time you've a mind to and that's where you'll find us.'

'We'll be speaking soon,' said Larssen, in such a tone as to suggest that the three of them would not exactly be sitting down to tea and chatting about the good old days at that next meeting.

8

Late on that Wednesday night, the Chicago headquarters of Pinkertons was humming with activity; messengers were coming and going and the telegraph line in the building was clacking away non-stop. The old man himself, who never seemed to need any sleep, was sitting in his private office, looking through a file that had only just arrived.

There was very little information about the train robbery and the little surprise that Pinkertons had planned for the robbers in Chris Mitford's office. His safe yielded nothing and all the business relating to it had been conducted by word of mouth. Somebody had had the idea of sending round to his apartment to see if he was keeping any papers appertaining to the matter there. This was an uncomfortable sort of undertaking, because his grieving widow was howling and bemoaning her fate all round the apartment, but when it was hinted that catching Mitford's murderer would be expedited by looking through his things, his wife was only too willing to accommodate them.

The handwritten notes which now lay on Alan Pinkerton's desk told the full story of Mitford's efforts to trap the Fraser brothers. There was an account of how he knew Dale Carnak and also the telegram that Carnak had sent from Jacksonville, alerting Mitford to the target of the attack and even giving him the day that it would take place.

Pinkerton was a very shrewd man and he could see at once why Mitford had kept this file at his home, rather than in the office. It could only be because he had it in mind to write young Carnak out of the script at some point; probably so that he wasn't obliged to share the glory with the man who had undertaken the most hazardous job of all, that of spy in the Fraser gang.

Taken together with some information which had just come to him by wire, these documents were enough to convince Pinkerton that he had been wrong about Dale Carnak. Examination of the site of the explosion showed that the charge had been set off by a fuse. It was impossible to think that this could have been timed to detonate just as the carriage containing his agents passed above it. Obviously, the hope was to stop the train and steal the silver. This Carnak had tipped off Mitford about the time and location of the robbery and then rode with the outlaws to be on the scene. That took a good deal of pluck and Alan Pinkerton felt ashamed of himself for having thought the man a villain. He decided then and there that if Dale Carnak pulled through, then the least he could do would be to offer him the job that that rogue Mitford had promised him.

Pinkerton was feeling very ill disposed towards the dead man that night. The file from his apartment had in it a copy of the specially doctored leaflet which Mitford had caused to be sent to the sheriff's office in Jacksonville and, it now appeared by some dreadful oversight, to twenty other sheriffs in Iowa. The good relationship that existed between the Pinkertons Agency and the official law was a delicate one. They traded information with each other, but this depended upon trust, which Alan Pinkerton had carefully nurtured over the years. If it became known that someone in his own headquarters had played some sheriff for a fool in this way, then it could do irreparable harm to the reputation of the Pinkertons Detective Agency.

There was another telegram from Carnak, delivered to Mitford via one of their cover addresses. Mitford's decoded version was clipped to it. It was brief and to the point, reading, 'Also part of it are Williams, Casey and Carter. Other names to follow.'

Pinkerton leaned back in his chair and lit a fat cigar; his only real vice these days. It was a terrible thing to wish for, but by far and away the neatest solution to the problem would be if young Dale Carnak were to be killed while on the run. That way, nobody would ever find out the trick that a Pinkerton man had pulled on the sheriff of Jacksonville.

It was curious that both Alan Pinkerton and the Fraser brothers should both be wishing for Carnak's speedy death as a way out of their difficulties. In his office in Jacksonville, however, Sheriff Orville Larssen was hoping for a very different outcome. He was very much of the opinion that the key to a number of mysteries that had been troubling him in the last few years might be held by the young man who had gone on the run that day.

After getting back to town after Carnak's escape, Larssen had gone for a little walk and asked a few seemingly casual questions of various people. He had done this not as official inquiries but more as a man who is trying to remember some trifling detail that is of no real importance but had been tugging at his attention.

His first port of call was at the offices of *The Jacksonville and Bartlow County Intelligencer and Weekly Record*, and the editor of the newspaper with whom he was on good terms. 'Jem,' he said to that worthy man when he found him cursing at the printers' errors with which that week's edition was littered, 'You recall a few weeks back when some young fellow stopped Seth Fraser from getting shot?'

'Sure I remember. We did a little filler about it, puffing up the county as the original home of the Rattlesnake Code. What of it?'

'You don't happen to call to mind his name, I suppose?'

''Course I do. It was an odd name, not one I ever come across before. Carnak. First or given name, Dale. Why?'

'You happen to know if Fraser saw him after that?'

'Yes, they were in the Broken Arrow a

few times and I saw them myself in the street. What gives, Orville? What's the story?'

'I can't say just for now. And I'd be mighty obliged to you, were you not to talk of this or ask me any more questions. But I tell you, it could be a big story and if so, I promise you that you will be the first to hear it and straight from me.'

'That's good enough for me. You and Hettie still coming by at the weekend?'

'I hope so, Jem. Unless we are overtaken by events.'

A brief chat in the Broken Arrow confirmed what he had already suspected, that Seth Fraser and Dale Carnak were as thick as thieves. Mind, Fraser had not actually said in as many words that he didn't know the man holding him and his brother at gunpoint, but that was without doubt the impression he was trying to give. Larssen had asked his deputy what he thought and he had looked at his boss as though he were going silly. He too took it for granted that Seth Fraser meant to convey that he had been bushwhacked by a stranger.

Now, sitting there in his office, Orville Larssen tried to put together the pieces of the puzzle. He had found the original leaflet from Pinkertons and now scrutinized it closely. Something about it was bothering him and it took a while before he could work out what it was.

The Pinkertons' circulars were beautifully constructed pieces of printing; laid out and produced by a man who took pride in his work. The headings were perfectly centred and the print justified neatly to one side on the body of the text. There was never a typo to be seen, nor, if it came to that, any ink smudges. The design and execution of the things would have done credit to a menu in a high class restaurant.

The one he held in his hand, though, was not quite perfect. There was something cramped and not altogether pleasing about the way that the piece about Dale Carnak was fitted into the other items. Then it struck Larssen all at once. Somebody had taken the original plates for the leaflet, removed some text and then inserted the bit about Carnak. That would account for the squashed look of that part. Having figured this out, the sheriff sat there for a minute or two longer, tapping his fingers on the desk top. The answer was clear enough now. Somebody at Pinkertons in Chicago wanted to spread the idea around that this Dale Carnak was a criminal with an interest in robbing trains. The only part he couldn't work out yet was why.

While Alan Pinkerton and Orville Larssen were sitting in comfortable offices, thinking about him, the object of their thoughts was himself crouched in a ditch on the edge of a stretch of farmland. He had tethered the horse nearby and what his next course of action was likely to be, the good Lord alone knew.

Not least of Carnak's problems were

the handcuffs which were chafing at his wrists and starting to make them sore. How he was going to rid himself of them, he had not faintest notion. Having his hands shackled together like this turned even the simplest of tasks into a tricky puzzle. He was not in immediate danger of being hanged, it was true, but those damned cuffs were like the mark of Cain; telling even the dullest-witted person that he was on the lam.

Well, there was nothing to be done about anything this day and that was for sure. Carnak looked around him at the ditch, which was lined with dried up old leaves. He had slept in worse places during the war. Nobody was shelling him here and as the ditch was dry, he kicked off his boots, lay them together and then settled back with his head resting upon them. He would just have to hope that he could come up with some plan in the morning.

The arrival of the 'special' in Claremont was an exciting event in that small town. The locomotive which drew into the railroad station at about five that afternoon was pulling only three coaches and was accordingly able to make astonishingly fast time from Chicago. One of the coaches carried fifteen hand-picked Pinkertons' agents and the other two carried their horses and tack. Once the little train stopped, the men were up and out of their carriage before the driver had even barely applied the brakes. The sight of fifteen horses trotting along the platform was a novel one and some of the passengers whose own train had been delayed to make way for this one, speculated that they were a troupe of circus riders. There was some excuse for thinking so, because these were men who liked to make a show of themselves.

Some of the men employed by Pinkertons were undercover operators; men who would fit in anywhere, without anybody guessing that they were lawmen. Others, though, like the men who arrived in Claremont that evening, made no secret of their profession and rode as proudly as soldiers in ceremonial dress. Some had intricately tooled holsters, others had silver charms hanging from their saddles or horse brasses or fancy spurs. These foppish little touches did not make them look any less menacing. For the first thought that struck most folk who crossed the path of these fellows was that it would be a very bad idea to get crosswise to them. You could see at a glance that they meant business and most who saw them were mighty glad that they were not the target of these men's enmity.

Alan Pinkerton was a man who would use a rapier or a bludgeon, depending upon circumstance. His agents could be as subtle as renaissance assassins or as crude as a Red Indian raiding party. It was all a question of what would serve best. In the present instance, there was to be no more pussyfooting around with the Fraser brothers. Everybody in the Pinkerton outfit was right ticked off with those two and now it was time for a reckoning; the day was approaching when somebody would have to pay for the murder of the fourteen agents during the bungled robbery.

The plan was that the Pinkerton's men would ride hard that very night along to Jacksonville. Once there, they would take the Fraser brothers one way or another. They just hoped that they got there before anybody else tackled them.

* * *

Sheriff Larssen had two more duties to perform that night before he went home to his wife. The first was to go down to the telegraph office and fire off a pretty sharp wire to Pinkertons, asking them straight out whether or not the leaflet about Dale Carnak had been a hoax to draw attention to him. Larssen was not a tactful or diplomatic man at the best of times and he didn't mince his words at all on this occasion.

After he had sent off the wire to Chicago, Larssen turned his steps towards the Broken Arrow, hoping to run to earth one of his deputies, Ted Baxter by name. Just as he had expected, Baxter was propping up the bar at the saloon, regaling a crowd of men with some smutty story. He smiled broadly when he caught sight of his boss, crying, 'Over here, Orville. Come and join the party.'

'Not this day, Ted. I hate to drag you away when you're having so much fun, but something's come up at the office. I wonder if you would favour me with your presence for a few minutes?'

'Ah shit,' said Baxter irritably, 'can't it wait 'til morning?'

'That it can't,' said Larssen definitely, a glint in his eye. 'We need to tackle it right now.'

'Ah well, if you say so. You boys wait up, now, I'll be back directly. You see how it is when you're a deputy and have a slave-driver like this as your boss?'

As the two men walked along the darkened street to the sheriff's office, Ted Baxter kept up a stream of cheerful remarks, which Larssen answered with non-committal grunts. Once they reached the office, Larssen opened the door and ushered the other man in first. Then he followed him inside, locking the door behind him. As he lit a lamp, he could sense Baxter staring at the back of his head, trying to make out the play.

When the office was flooded with the warm yellow light of the oil lamp, Sheriff Larssen sat down and indicated for his deputy to take the other chair. When the man was settled, Larssen said, 'It's all up, Ted. I know what's been going on.'

'You say what?' asked Baxter, his face a mask of puzzled innocence. 'What is it that you say's been going on, Orville?'

'Do we have to go through it all?' asked the sheriff wearily, 'can't you just hand me that star on your shirt and be done with it? I ain't blaming you or nothing. As far as I'm concerned, all I want is for you to leave this job.'

'I tell you now, you better be able to back this up,' said Baxter in a tight, ugly voice. 'I ain't about to leave this job without a fight. It pays better than labouring in a field and I do it right good, as well you know.'

'Ted, it's up to you. I know now for certain sure that you've been passing information out of this office in exchange for money. Any fool can see that you spend more than your salary's worth. I knew you were on the take in some way, but never could figure out how. Until tonight, that is.'

Baxter began to bluster and raise his voice, but Larssen cut him off short by raising his hand and saying, 'We do it the easy way or the hard way. It's up to you and I tell you now, I don't give a shit which way you choose. The easy way is you handing over that badge and leaving my employ. The hard way involves me arresting you for misconduct in public office, bribery and

153

suchlike. Which'll you have?'

The deputy sat for a moment or two, considering the options, then asked quietly, 'How'd you find out?'

Larssen shrugged, greatly relieved that they would be able to deal with the thing without any unpleasantness. 'I noticed a while back how some of the robberies in this part of the state, stages and railroad trains both, were very neatly targeted just where there was something special to be had. It wasn't hard to see that somebody was very well informed. It all came together today. You've been passing on all the information in those Pinkertons' circulars we get.'

'A man has to look after himself, Orville. I got two littl'uns to raise.'

'Ah, get out of my sight. You make me sick!'

Larssen got up to unlock the street door. As Ted Baxter passed out of the office, the sheriff said casually, 'I suppose it was the Frasers you was giving all our stuff to?'

'Yeah. That's right. So long, Orville.'

This question had been the whole and entire object of the exercise and until Baxter answered, all Sheriff Larssen had had were suspicions and a vague feeling of unease. Now he knew.

Like many people, he had wondered about how come the Frasers were doing so well out of their farm. His private guesses before this day ran to moonshining or perhaps running guns to the Indians. He would never have suspected them of being road agents. For better than two years they had plied their trade right under his nose and he had not even noticed. It was not until that little comedy today when they were pretending to be the victims of a robbery themselves that he had even thought of them in that connection.

What had they been doing before they started down this road? Although they lived with their mother, both men were absent from the family home for greater or lesser periods of time. Had they been going off to other parts of the country to commit their crimes? Not that it mattered. Most likely, once they were both under lock and key, there would be time to look into that sort of thing before they were hanging for the recent murders.

9

Thursday, 14 April dawned bright and clear. Carnak was woken by the cheerful twittering of birds in the trees which surrounded the nearby farm. He was aching and stiff, his manacled wrists having made it all but impossible to lie comfortably during the night. He sat up and stretched. The first thing to do was hunt out something to eat. He realized that it was more than a day since he had filled his belly properly.

There was no sign of life around the stone-built farmhouse which was on the other side of the field from where he had spent the night. It might be worth trying to beg a crust, if it wasn't for these damned gyves. First person to clap eyes upon him was going to go running off to lay an information with the nearest sheriff's office for sure.

Carnak got to his feet and realized

that he was that hungry, he felt a little faint. This wouldn't answer; he would have to get some vittles, even if it was just some raw vegetables. Nigh to the farmhouse was what looked like a little kitchen garden. Would there be anything worth eating at this time of year? He wasn't a farmer, but he had an idea that the chances were slender. Still and all, there was nothing else to be done. He scrambled out of the ditch and set off over the field. When he was fifteen feet from the little vegetable patch, an old man came out of the house. He was carrying a double-barrelled scattergun, which he raised to his shoulder and proceeded to point at Carnak.

'Don't shoot, mister,' said Carnak, 'I mean you no harm.'

'Mean me no harm, hey?' said the man. 'What for are you skulking round my house, then? Hey? Just answer me that.'

'I'm hungry is all,' Carnak told him. 'I have not ate properly since the day before yesterday.'

'What's to do with the chains? You an escaped prisoner?'

'It's a long story — '

'I'll be bound it is. Tell me straight, have you fell foul of the law?'

'You might say so,' said Carnak, not feeling in the mood to discuss his life with a stranger. He wondered what the next stage would be — this old fellow locking him in a barn while he fetched assistance?

In fact, what happened next was most surprising, because the old man put down his gun by leaning it against a cherry tree and said, 'Come over to yon barn, now. Don't be afeared, I'm no great fan of the law myself. Come on, now.'

Hardly able to believe the evidence of his senses, Carnak followed the man to see what would chance next.

The inside of the barn was gloomy and dark. In the centre of it stood a sawn-off tree stump, surrounded by split logs. The man went over to the wall and picked up a heavy-looking axe.

He gestured for Carnak to come closer and then said, 'Here now, we'll have you free in next to no time. Just set your hands on this here stump.'

Carnak looked dubiously at the section of some tree. The idea of putting his hands on there and letting this man swing an axe down on them was not an appealing one. 'What's the matter?' said the old man, as though he could read Carnak's mind, 'you yellow? Or you think I'm too old to swing this axe without chopping off your hand? Come now, before I change my mind and send for the sheriff.'

Very slowly and with the greatest reluctance, Carnak laid his hands on the block, stretching the chain between the handcuffs as hard as he could, so as to give the man with the axe as much space as possible. The man spat on his hands and said, 'Ready, now? Don't you flinch or move, mind, 'cause you're apt to lose one of your hands.' He raised the axe high above his head and brought it down with tremendous force, severing the chain that linked the two parts of the handcuffs.

Carnak stretched his arms; it was a great relief to be free of the constriction. He rubbed his wrists.

'Chafing, hey?' said the man, 'I know how it feels, son. Lookee here, I have some rags in this box. We can wrap them round those irons, so's they won't rub so. Stop folk seeing them, too, which is always a good idea.'

As the old man helped him, Carnak said, 'You seem to know a lot about these things, meaning handcuffs and such.'

'Happen I do, boy, happen I do. I was in the penitentiary for better than fifteen years. Learned a lot about chains and so on in that place.'

At a guess, thought Carnak, fifteen years in the pen meant murder or manslaughter. He didn't wish to know, though. It was enough that he could now move about a little more freely.

'You say you're hungry?' asked the man, 'I reckon I could rustle up some

161

eggs if that would suit?'

'It surely would, sir, I would be very grateful.'

'Ain't no call to 'sir' me. My name's Jethro. That'll do.'

After a plate of eggs, half a loaf of bread and a pot of coffee, Carnak felt more like a human being and less like a hunted animal. He knew very well what his next move was going to be and felt somewhat ashamed of it. Not that there was much choice in the matter. He stood up and said to the old man, 'You have been right good to me and I don't like to give you a base return, but needs must, you know. I'm a going to borrow that scattergun of yours. I will return it when I am able.'

Without waiting to see what Jethro would say to this proposal, Carnak marched out of the kitchen and snatched up the gun where it was leaning against the tree. As the old man emerged from the farmhouse, Carnak held the gun to his hip and shook his head warningly. Jethro did not seem at all put out or even surprised by this turn of events. 'Son of a bitch,' he exclaimed wonderingly. 'You'd take my best scattergun on top of everything. Son of a bitch!'

Carnak felt himself to be a rare scoundrel for treating the fellow so, but thought that he detected a note of reluctant admiration in the old boy's tone, rather than anger. Maybe he had expected Carnak to take his gun. When he had reached the other side of the field, Carnak turned to see Jethro still standing there, shaking his head. Carnak shouted, 'I'll return it when I have finished with it.'

'Mind you do!' called the old man in reply and waved in a friendly enough fashion.

He's a strange one and no mistake, thought Carnak to himself as he collected his horse and set off towards the rising sun. He figured he was south of Jacksonville by a few miles and unless he missed his guess, the Frasers lived in one of the farms hereabouts.

At the same time that Carnak left old man Jethro's place, the Fraser brothers were sitting at the old oak table in the kitchen of their childhood home, eating breakfast. The little servant girl scuttled around, mostly out in the yard or attending to their mother's needs, but from time to time fussing about in the kitchen. When she was in the room with them, Seth and Dan limited their talk to agricultural matters and then when she left, they resumed talking about their more urgent concerns.

'You felt the same as me,' said Seth, 'that Orville Larssen was looking at us oddly?'

'You spoke too much,' said Dan briefly, 'as was often your trouble as a boy. Like as not, Larssen has seen us in Carnak's company. He'll be like a terrier on a rat now, trying to fathom out the game.'

At this point, Mary-Anne came in from the garden with a bundle of kindling wood. She began arranging this neatly by the hearth in a maddeningly slow and precise way. After she had been fooling around with the stuff for a few minutes, Seth said, 'Mary-Anne, you might leave that and go up to my mother and see if she needs anything.'

The girl hurried from the room. Dan said, 'What do you say we should do?'

'Ride out and see the boys,' said Seth at once. 'Make sure that they're all back home and remind them to keep their mouths shut. There's nothing to connect us with that crime and if we all hold our nerve, why, then there's nothing to fret over.'

'I mind that young Jake Carter will need a specially firm word.'

'Leave him to me.'

After a little more conversation, touching upon the most likely of their gang to start opening their mouths and blabbing and the methods to be used to discourage the same, the Fraser brothers went up to bid their ma good morning and farewell for the day. The old woman was not in the best of moods.

'Well then,' she greeted them, 'what

mischief have you been up to now? Don't bother lying to me. Your guilt's written across your faces as plain as plain.'

'Ma,' said Seth, trying to sooth and placate his mother, 'don't take on so. We are going to visit our neighbours. There's no mischief in the case.'

'Don't talk to me,' said old Mrs Fraser, 'I saw that you boys would be a torment, the day you was born. I bore it well, but after all these years, it is wearing me down.'

Dan said, 'Is there aught we can get you before we leave? Something from the kitchen, perhaps?'

'Do you think I'm a child?' she inquired. 'You think giving me a biscuit will take my mind away from what I am after? Nothing of the sort. I knowed you two was young limbs of Satan when you was boys and you ain't changed at all since. Still up to all manner of wickedness. Well, that's the cross a mother has to bear.'

After they had taken their leave, Seth

said to his brother, 'She ain't going to take overmuch to it when we have to go a bit further afield. It would be madness to carry out any more games round here now, what with Larssen suspicious.'

'Meaning we'll be away from home for a whiles, soon?' asked Dan. 'Yes, Ma won't like that, I will grant you.'

As the Frasers were riding out from their farm, the fifteen men from Pinkertons were arriving in Jacksonville from Claremont. They were travel-stained and weary, but still cut somewhat of a dash as they trotted down Main Street. One of the peculiarities of men like these, who did not engage in undercover work, was that they almost all grew luxuriant and ostentatious mustaches, which made them look a little like cavalrymen. In combination with their fancy saddles and holsters, they were certainly a sight to catch the eye as they entered Jacksonville that morning.

Two of the eyes they caught belonged

to Sheriff Larssen, who could smell trouble fifty miles off. As soon as he set eyes on these boys, Larssen knew that they were birds of ill omen. There was a convention that Pinkerton's men always notified the official law when they were planning to carry out some operation in or near a town. Orville Larssen, who could see at once who these men were, did not propose to sit and wait for them to come calling at his office and so he watched them from the sidewalk, to see which way they would go. As he had suspected, they reined in outside the saloon, maybe with the hope of having breakfast and washing the trail dirt from their mouths. Larssen followed on foot at a leisurely and unhurried pace.

The men were all lined up at the bar, which in the normal way of things would hardly have opened yet. Howsoever, the owner scented the possibility of a good bit of business and so was busy out back cooking up some food for these boys. Larssen strolled up to the nearest man and introduced himself. 'Tell me now,' he said, 'who might be in charge here?'

'That'd be me,' said a tall, rangy-looking individual with iron-grey hair; although he could scarcely have been more than thirty. 'You would be Sheriff Larssen. We was fixing to come by your office and visit later.'

'Were you?' replied Larssen pleasantly, 'well that's right nice of you. Suppose we just cut the crap and talk about what you men are doing round here. I'll warrant you're from Pinkertons.'

'You got that right, Sheriff,' said the leader in a faintly mocking tone, 'that is very observant of you.'

Sheriff Larssen walked over to the man who had spoken and said, 'I wouldn't advise anybody in this town to get fresh with me. It will not answer. That goes as much for visitors as it does for the folk who live here all the time. What are you here for?'

'There was a bunch of men killed up north of here on the railroad. Most of them was our comrades and we aim to find those responsible.'

'You know,' said Larssen, still in that pleasant, even voice, 'now I come to think of it, I have a crow to pluck with you Pinkerton's boys. It relates to a forged notice inserted in one of your leaflets. I don't suppose any of you would know what I'm talking about?'

The leader of the men said helpfully, 'It was perhaps a different department, Sheriff. We are a big organization and each of us can't know all that goes on.'

'I will tell you this once for all,' said the sheriff, 'you men have no more power and authority here than any other private citizen. I know that in some towns they let you throw your weight around like you was real lawmen. Well this is not one of those places, you see. Here, I am the law and if I see anybody muscling in on my jurisdiction, I am liable to get ratty. Do we understand each other?'

The Pinketons' man, who had prior to this been disposed to dismiss Larssen as some no-count hick over whom he could ride roughshod, said, 'Why don't you and me step out into the street a moment, Sheriff, and talk turkey?'

Once he was away from his men, the leader of the Pinkertons' agents introduced himself as Pete Relph. 'Nobody wants to tread on your toes,' he said to Larssen, 'but we are resolved to catch the men who carried out that massacre. We will hand them over to you when we got them. Nothing could be fairer. Only, you see, our boss is most particular that it should be us as catches them and not anybody else. You might call it a matter of honour.'

'Some places,' remarked Sheriff Larssen, 'have vigilance committees which run alongside the sheriff's office and even override the sheriff if they feel the need. There's nothing like that round here and I wouldn't have it. Any arrests made within ten miles of Jacksonville and I am the one to make them.'

Relph stirred and looked uneasy at this, but the sheriff continued. 'That don't mean that you and me can't work together agreeable. I'm sure we can. I will ride along with you and your men and be there when any arrests are made. I owe that to the town.'

Pete Relph thought about this for a space and then said, 'We ain't a lynching party, you know.'

'Never said you were. I don't take too kindly to men being roughed up when they're caught or anything in that line, neither. Here's how the land lies. Either I come with you or you set yourself against me and I will summon aid to disarm you all.'

'Well, Sheriff, you are a real hard bargainer, but I think you have a deal. Will you join us now so that I can explain to the boys how it is?'

The two men went back into the Broken Arrow as amiable and friendly as could be, although inwardly Relph was cursing the sheriff's family back for several generations and calling him a variety of unflattering names.

* * *

Dave Casey was not best pleased to see the Frasers turn up at his place early that Thursday. He had been trying to forget all about the killings in which he had taken his part and get back to tending his fields.

Seth and Dan Fraser could be mighty disconcerting when the mood was upon them. That's how it was today. They sat there on their horses, away across the fields; just watching him at work for a spell. After a few minutes of this, with neither of them waving or otherwise signalling, just setting there immobile like Indians, Casey had had enough. He threw down his tools and walked over to the two of them. As he approached, the two men just sat there, staring at him expressionlessly. It surely was off-putting when the Fraser brothers were like this.

'Hey, fellows,' said Casey, 'What's to do?'

'We was wondering,' said Dan, in a flat, cold voice, 'if you had been running off at the mouth about our late adventures?'

A chill of fear ran through Casey. 'No, of course not. You know I wouldn't talk out of turn like that. You both know that.'

'I tell you this now,' said Dan, 'if we should be suspicioned over this, then I am apt to be very aggravated. So if you was thinking of chatting, turning state's evidence or anything else, you can be very sure that I will get to you. Even in gaol.'

'Shit, there ain't no call to talk so . . . ' began Casey, but he was speaking to the wind. Seth and Dan had whirled their horses round and had cantered off. Casey found that although it was a chill morning, his shirt was sticking to his side, clammy with perspiration.

The next port of call was Jake Carter, but it was there that the Frasers received a big shock and the realization began to dawn on them that things might be falling apart for them. Marion Carter informed them that she hadn't seen hide nor hair of her husband since Monday.

'Any idea where he was going, Ma'am?' asked Seth in a casual and friendly way.

'He don't never much tell me anything about his business. Just ups and goes when he will.'

When they were back on the road, Seth remarked to his brother, 'Something's amiss, you know that? What say we go and see one of the others who went off with Carter. Who were the other two?'

'Williams and Wright,' said Dan, 'but we need not bother. Something has miscarried.'

Nevertheless, they went to see if Tom Wright was home, only to be told the same tale by his wife; that she hadn't seen her husband since the Monday.

'Only question is,' said Dan, after they had left, 'whether they talked before they died.'

'What, you think they been killed by vigilance men?'

'Or died in a gun battle, which would be better; not allowing them the chance to beg for their lives by offering our names to the lynching party.'

The Fraser brothers rode on soberly. Neither of them said it out loud, but it was beginning to look increasingly likely that they would have to leave their ma to the care of the servants for a few months, while they went off and waited for the heat to die down a little.

* * *

Alan Pinkerton had repented of his wish to see Dale Carnak dead just to save him a little embarrassment. It would be a scurvy trick to play on the young man; to leave him for the wolves just so that he, Alan Pinkerton, would not have to explain that not all his employees were up to scratch. Once again, he cursed the memory of Christopher Mitford.

On the old man's desk that Thursday morning was a telegram addressed directly to him, which showed that even disowning Carnak would not avoid the need for some apologies. The telegram was from the sheriff of Jacksonville and it inquired as to whether the head of the Pinkertons Detective Agency was aware that one of his men had been sending false information out to a sheriff's office. The name 'Dale Carnak' jumped out of the text at once.

Pinkerton might be as hard as nails and a real Tartar to work for, but he was essentially a decent and honourable man. It would be a poor trick to play on the young man after he had risked his life, believing himself to be working for Pinkertons. He had showed more mettle that some of the genuine agents and the least that could be done was to extricate him from his current pinch and offer him a job with the company.

Accordingly, Alan Pinkerton scribbled a couple of messages, one to Sheriff Larssen and the other for Pete Relph, and then rang for the office boy. When he knocked and entered the inner sanctum, the old man handed him the paper and said, 'Quick as you like, Jimmy. I want these to reach Jacksonville yesterday!'

10

After relieving old Jethro of his scattergun, Dale Carnak thought that there was no purpose in delaying matters further and that he might just as well head over to the Frasers' farm and take them in to Jacksonville. Surely, that would show whose side he was on? He hoped that a wire to Pinkertons would clear up any misunderstanding about his status, as to whether he was an outlaw or a Pinkertons agent.

He knew that the Fraser brothers lived south of Jacksonville, but that was the sum total of his knowledge and so he set off to find somebody who might direct him on the right road. It did not take too long to find a man hedging and ditching who was able to point out the best way of getting to the Fraser place. He eyed Carnak's gun with some trepidation and it struck Carnak that the night he had spent in a ditch probably had not improved his appearance any. I reckon, he thought to himself, that I have 'escaped outlaw' writ all over me.

The Fraser place, when he came to it, was not a whole lot different from the other farmhouses scattered across this part of the country around Jacksonville. It was perhaps a little larger and better maintained, but that was all. Carnak rode into the yard and saw a pretty girl of about eighteen or nineteen, who was hanging clothes out on a line. He called out to her, 'Excuse me, Miss?'

'Nobody's at home,' she said. 'The masters have gone off, who knows where. There's only me here. And the Mistress, of course.'

Carnak dismounted and strolled over to the girl. She watched him nervously; he could tell that she was unsure of his intentions. 'I mean you no harm,' said Carnak, 'but I could do with a cup of water.'

'Come into the scullery, then. We

have a pitcher of cold milk if you would prefer it.'

'Thank you. Thank you very much.'

The kitchen was stone-flagged and cool. Here too, one could see that there was plenty of money being spent, although not in a gaudy or ostentatious way. There was a wooden dresser with beautiful china and the walls were lined with copper pans and kitchen utensils. From somewhere in the house, came a querulous voice, 'Mary-Anne, who you got down there? I hear you talking in the yard.'

'I best go up. Don't you meddle with anything.'

The girl came down again after a minute and said, 'Mistress wants to speak to you. Says she ain't spoke to a stranger for a good long while. Lord knows what her boys will say.'

The servant led Carnak through the hall and up the stairs. She knocked at a door, which was already open, and a woman's voice said, 'Don't hover on the threshold, there. Just step right in.'

Carnak was still clutching the old man's gun and he was worried that this would give him an aggressive appearance and maybe frighten the old lady sitting up in the double bed. She marked the weapon and eyed Carnak narrowly, but did not seem to be scared by him. Instead she said, 'That's all, Mary-Anne. You can leave us now.'

The girl sketched a hasty curtsy and withdrew.

'You're no pedlar,' said the woman and then, before he had time to deny or confirm this statement, she said, 'you ain't the law, neither. What are you, bounty killer?'

'My name is Dale Carnak, ma'am.'

'Well I'm no further forward for knowing it,' she replied tartly, 'now I know your name, or what you say's your name. Still don't know what you're after. You know who I am?'

'I guess that you're Mrs Fraser,' hazarded Carnak, 'Seth and Dan's mother.'

'Right in one. Are you a friend of my sons?'

'No,' said Carnak, 'I ain't exactly that.'

'You come to kill 'em, then?'

'Lord forbid, I ain't a killer.'

' 'Lord forbid' is pious enough, but it don't tell me much. Come, out with it, what do you want?'

'I come to take your boys to the law in Jacksonville.'

'What for?'

'I don't like to talk of such things to a lady. They have done bad things, ma'am.'

'How bad? Robbing?'

'Yes, ma'am.'

'Murder?'

'Yes, that too.'

There was silence for a time and then the old woman said, 'Go over to yonder bureau, there by the window.' Carnak did so. 'Now open that top drawer and take out a black leather bag that lays there. You see it?'

He pulled out a stout leather bag with a shiny brass catch. Mrs Fraser said, 'Fetch it over here now.' When he did so, she said, 'I keep my money in here, for paying household accounts and suchlike.' She pulled out a bundle of bills and leafed through them. 'There's nearly five hundred dollars here. It's yours, if you'll just ride off now and forget about my sons.'

There was no earthly reason why Carnak should not take this money and just disappear; forget about the Frasers and use the cash to make a new start somewhere. Even so, he hesitated for only a heartbeat, before saying, 'No, I can't do that. I'm sorry.'

'They was always bad, you know. Even as little ones, they had the Devil in them. I tried to whip it out, but made no odds. Soon as I stopped, they'd be off out and up to some other mischief. They ain't changed, but they're still my boys.'

'I'm sorry,' said Carnak, 'I must go. I'm sorry to be the cause of any misfortune, but I aim to take your sons anyway.' He left the room, sorry for the woman and maybe a little vexed at himself for refusing the money.

The Frasers visited every member of their little band and found that only Williams, Carter and Wright had failed to make it back to their homes. This made it a racing certainty that some ill had befallen them and both the brothers prayed fervently that this might have been death, rather than arrest. Arrested men, especially if they are facing the noose, tend to talk a lot and offer all manner of information to save their own lives. As they headed back to their farm, Seth said to his brother, 'I reckon we should dig up for a space and go south. Maybe Texas. There's enough money to make sure Ma will be took care of and we can engage servants to live at the house. It won't be the first time we've had to leave her for a while.'

'She ain't getting any younger,' observed Dan, to which his brother replied, 'No and we won't grow any older if we get caught over that robbery, neither. They'll hang us for sure.'

They carried on for a while down the road and then Seth said, 'Hush, I can hear horses, many of them.'

They were riding along a short cut to their home; a little track that led along the side of a hill and avoided the road. They could see the road from this track, though, and as they watched, better than a dozen heavily armed riders swept along the road, going in the same direction as their farm.

The two brothers sat perfectly still, hoping that none of the horsemen would glance up and to their right, and so see them sitting there on the hillside. None of them did and the troop of riders was soon hidden by the trees that lined the road further down.

'If that weren't a posse, then I never seed one,' remarked Seth Fraser judicially, as though the fact did not mean life and death to him.

'I reckon as you're right about that,' said Dan, 'meaning I suppose that we'll need to be leaving sooner rather than later.'

'It'll blow over in time. There's nothing against us, save their suspicions. Six months' time, the whole thing'll be forgot.'

'We'd best stay low for a few hours, give those boys time to search our house and then go back to Jacksonville,' said Dan.

'Lucky we chose this morning for paying our social calls, all things taken into account.'

'Ain't that the truth!'

The two of them made their way swiftly to the wood which crowned the hill around which they had been riding. From there, there was a good view of the countryside for some good distance all around. They could not see the road directly from this vantage point, but would be able to hear the hoofs of the riders as they returned to Jacksonville, thus signalling that the coast was clear for them to return to their home.

The arrival of sixteen fierce and determined looking riders at the Fraser farm threw Mary-Anne into something approaching a panic. She was only saved from a nervous collapse by the intervention of Sheriff Larssen, whom she knew by sight from her shopping trips to Jacksonville. 'Come now, girl,' said Larssen, 'there's nothing to be alarmed about, you're not in trouble. We are looking to speak to Seth and Dan. Are they here?'

'No, sir,' replied the scared girl. 'They went out earlier and are not yet back. You're not the first to be asking after them, though.'

'Are we not?' said Larssen with interest. 'Who else has been here, then?'

'Well, he didn't leave his name. But he was young. And he had a gun.'

'Lot of men carry guns, you know,' said the sheriff gently, trying to reassure the girl.

'Yes, but they generally have them in holsters. This man was carrying a double-barrelled thing under his arm, like he might be going to use it in a hurry.'

'Did he, by God? Can you tell me what he looked like?'

The girl gave a description which could easily have matched Dale Carnak.

Sheriff Larssen caught Pete Relph's eye and raised his eyebrows expressively. Then he said to the servant, 'Now then, what's your name?'

'Mary-Anne, sir.'

'Well, Mary-Anne, we are going to have to look round the house here, to make sure that those two fellows are really not at home.'

'I wouldn't tell a story!' said Mary-Anne indignantly.

'I don't suppose you would,' said Larssen, 'but I have my work to do, just as you have yours. In this case, my job is to search for Seth and Dan Fraser. I suppose their mother is at home?'

'I don't know if she'll take kindly to having her house searched.'

'Tell you what,' said the sheriff, dismounting, 'me and this here chap, whose name is Pete, will come and wait downstairs, while you run up and tell her we'd like a few words.'

Pete Relph and Larssen followed the girl into the kitchen and then waited there as she went upstairs. Relph said,

'We're going to look pretty damned silly if those boys come bursting out now and shoot us down. You ask me, we should have brought some more men in here.'

'You could tell as well as me that that child wasn't telling us any lies. We'll look in every room and even under the beds if it'll make you feel any better, but I'd take oath that the Fraser brothers aren't here.'

'Let's hope you're right.'

Mary-Anne came down and said, 'Mistress says to go on up.' She led them upstairs and ushered them into the old woman's bedroom.

'Good day to you, Mrs Fraser,' said Sheriff Larssen. 'You're looking very well. It is a while since we met.'

'You ain't improved with age, Orville Larssen. I recall you as a boy. You always were a little goody two-shoes. Being sheriff is just the sort of job for a man like you, spending your days poking your big nose into other folks' business.'

Larssen said, 'That's as may be, Ma'am. It was really your sons that we were hoping to see. Do you know where they are?'

'I don't, and even if I did, I wouldn't be telling you. There, what do you say to that?'

'Only that I dare say you won't mind us looking round?'

'What for? Don't take my word for it?'

'Mrs Fraser,' said Larssen patiently, 'your sons are suspected of involvement in a serious crime. I wouldn't be doing my duty if I didn't look for them.'

'Oh, go on then,' said Mrs Fraser, 'get on and turn the house upside down. You'll not find them, because they ain't here.'

As he and Pete Relph left the room, Sheriff Larssen paused at the door and turned back to the woman who sat in the bed, glaring at them. He said, 'I remark that you have not asked us what your boys are wanted for. That's strange.'

She snorted. 'It's no mystery. The young man that was here said something about robbery and murder. He was a polite young fellow with an honest open face. Not a sly-boots like you, Larssen.'

As they gave the house a cursory examination, Relph said to the sheriff, 'The old lady didn't seem to care much for you.'

'She never did, even when I was a boy. Her own boys were so much trouble to her, she couldn't bear it when she saw others who behaved well. Saw it as a reproach, maybe.'

'Was that you then, Larssen? One of the boys who behaved well?'

'We got better things to do than talk of my childhood,' said Larssen. 'Let's get out of here and work out the way to proceed.'

* * *

After leaving the Fraser place, Dale Carnak was at a loss to know how to go about things. On the one hand, he did not want to ride around too much, drawing attention to himself. He was, after all, a fugitive from the law; at least technically. Then again, he did not wish to hang round too long, just waiting for the Frasers to show up. When they met, he wanted it to be upon his own terms and to have plenty of forewarning so that he could make his plans.

The solution was simple and he smiled when it came to him. There was no work being done on the fields of the Frasers' farm this day, but away over yonder was a barn. He could see that it had a hay loft with a little winch near the roof and a door to swing bales in and out of. It might make the perfect spot to hole up for a few hours.

The barn was just right for Carnak's purposes. His horse would be happy there for a while and he himself could settle down on the hay. He had a strong notion that even when they did come back, the Frasers would not be engaging in any sort of agricultural work that day and so there would probably be no occasion for anybody to disturb him. Anyway, he was a light sleeper and being up in the hay loft with the scattergun near to hand, he thought he was as safe as he could hope for.

So it was that when the Pinkerton's men turned up at the Fraser farm with Sheriff Larssen, Dale Carnak was enjoying a refreshing slumber only a short distance away.

Once they were out of the Fraser's house, Pete Relph said to Larssen, 'Well, how do you want to play it? I thought about leaving three men here to watch the place. Then we could all go back to town and rest up. Those fellows aren't going to come home with us stamping about like this. They're fly boys all right. Anybody can operate right under your nose like that for years has got to be pretty sharp.'

'You could say so,' replied Larssen, a little bitterly. 'You'd have thought I would have paid them more heed. I knew they weren't getting all their income from this farm. Just thought it was something a little lighter than armed robbery, is all.'

'What do you say then? Is it all right with you if I tell three of my boys to hide up and then race over to tell us if the Frasers show up?'

'I can't think of any better plan, offhand,' said the sheriff.

When Larssen and the rest of the Pinkerton's men got back to town, the first thing that both he and Pete Relph had in mind was to go down to the telegraph office to see if there was anything waiting for them there. Both men had a message and both were from Alan Pinkerton in person. Larssen's was a fulsome apology and an admission that one of his men had tried to fool the sheriff. It ended by asking Larssen to look out for one Dale Carnak who, contrary to the information he had been sent a couple of weeks back, was in fact an employee of the Pinkertons Detective Agency.

The telegram to Pete Relph told him

to do his best to be nice to the sheriff in Jacksonville and to try to find Dale Carnak and bring him back safely to Chicago; not as a prisoner, but as a fellow agent.

When they had finished reading their telegrams, the two men looked at each other and then, without a word, each handed the other their own message. By the time that they had both read the two telegrams, Larssen and Relph knew where they stood. Their two aims coincided in every particular; to catch the Frasers and find Dale Carnak.

Sheriff Larssen declined Relph's offer of a drink, it still being early afternoon, and instead went back to his office, which was being tended by his other deputy, Cal Waters. Cal was not alone in the office when Larssen got there. Marion Carter was there, demanding that something was done to track down her husband who, she said, had now been missing for three days.

Cal seemed to be somewhat over-whelmed by the woman and so Larssen decided to take charge of the situation. 'Mrs Carter,' he said firmly, 'your husband is a grown person. I can't go off hunting for every man that takes off for a few days like that.'

'I'm afeared as some ill has befallen Jake,' she said. 'I don't know what he was up to, but he was nervous about it before he went. Then those Frasers come by, asking for him today. Seemed to think he ought to be back by now.'

'The Frasers?' said Larssen quickly. 'You mean Seth and Dan?'

'Yes, who else?'

'Is your husband a friend of theirs?'

'Not a friend, exactly,' said Marion Carter. 'They go off together at odd times. Maybe every two months. Sometimes more, sometimes less.'

After getting rid of Marion Carter by promising to look into her husband's whereabouts, Larssen said to Cal Waters, 'Cal, we are going to need some assistance. Can I look to you to raise six or seven men to ride tomorrow? Not hotheads, but steady fellows as will do as they are bid.'

'Sure, you want I should start now? What's it all about?'

'What it's about is that I am starting to think that those who killed all those men up on the railroad line between Barnard's Crossing and Claremont all come from hereabouts.'

'The hell they do! What makes you think so, boss?'

'Some of it's no more than a hunch. But tomorrow, I want to ride round and speak to a few people. Not like a casual chat, but with a bunch of men. I want it to scare those we see.'

Having set this in motion, Larssen went over to the Broken Arrow to see how Pete Relph was doing.

★ ★ ★

When Seth and Dan heard the rumble of hoofs passing along the nearby road in the direction of Jacksonville, they did not at once set off for their home. They were too wily for that by far. Instead, they sat and smoked for better than an hour. Their conversation during this time, although desultory, did not stray far from the business in hand.

'Ma'll be wild,' said Seth, 'when she learns we are going away again, I mean.'

'I guess she'd sooner we went for a while and then came back again, rather than stay and be hanged,' Dan remarked, which was very likely true.

They said nothing more for ten minutes and then Dan said, 'Reckon any of those boys we rode with in Texas are still on the scout?'

'Shouldn't think so,' replied his brother shortly. 'I reckon they will all have hanged or been shot by now.'

'It's a shame about that train,' said Dan. 'Had we pulled that one off, we could have gone for a good time without doing any more jobs at all.'

'Yes, that's often the way. You make plans and then they don't come off.'

Conversations of this kind were the closest that the Frasers ever came to reflecting deeply on their lives and thinking about the nature of the world in general. Neither of them spoke again for a quarter hour and then Dan broke the silence by observing, 'I'd like to kill that Carnak. Can you believe it, him working for Pinkertons all along?'

'Yes, that was a facer and no mistake. You blame me for drawing him in?'

'Hell no, we both thought he was all right,' said Dan, 'I just wish I would get the opportunity to shoot him, is all.'

They said nothing more for half an hour and then Seth stretched and said, 'Well, I reckon we might be getting home and packing a few things. We can leave instructions with that girl. There are a few men who owe us favours and who can see about getting servants and so on to look after Ma.'

'Come on,' said Dan, 'let's get to the house before that posse shows up again.'

11

Three men had been left behind to stake out the Frasers' farm and watch for their return. The difficulty was that while it is easy enough for a man to hide in some small space beneath a hedge or up in a tree, the same is not true of his horse. There was precious little good in leaving men there who would simply see the Frasers returning home. The whole point of the scheme was that once this happened, a messenger could ride swiftly to Jacksonville and summon the rest of the Pinkertons' agents to descend upon the farmhouse.

One man, Larry Davis, had chosen to leave his horse some distance away on the other side of a stand of trees and to secrete himself behind a stone wall near the house. He was careful to avoid being seen by the young girl, who came in and out of the yard at intervals. From his position, he could see the house and yard and unless you were looking straight at him, you would not have been able to guess he was there, as only the very top of his head showed above the wall. There were bushes behind him, which also helped with his camouflage.

One of the other men had taken up his watch on a rise of ground, some way from the house, with his horse left on the other side of the rise. This fellow lay flat on the very top of the hillock, so that he offered no outline against the sky. The third and final watcher was a little further than the other two, and hiding in plain view, as you might say. He was riding up and down the road leading to Jacksonville; first going one way and then the other. He thought that anybody seeing him would take him for a chance traveller. This might have worked if it had not been that as they walked their horses from the wood, Seth Fraser saw this fellow

201

heading along the road to their house. A short time later, he was heading back again; not having had time in between to have gone anywhere.

'Dan,' said Seth to his brother, 'that man who just rode along the road there. He was travelling the other way a minute or two back. Why,' he exclaimed sharply, 'there he is again, now heading this way.'

'He's setting a watch on the house,' said Dan grimly. 'Like as not, he's not the only one, neither.'

'We'd best take him then. No shooting, though. Could be that gun-shots will be signals for others to come and see what's what.'

The track that the brothers were on was high above the road and disappeared into some trees that lined it. It was into these trees that the rider went every few minutes, before emerging again shortly afterwards.

The Frasers trotted down to the road after the man had turned once more and gone off towards their house. They then proceeded at a walk in the same direction, confident that before long, the fellow would have turned back once more and be heading towards them. Sure enough, just as they entered the tunnel formed by the trees which overhung the road at this point, here he came, heading straight for them.

The rider who approached them was skilled at his work; they would have to give him that. Despite the fact that he would have been given their description and therefore knew at once who they were, he gave no sign, just nodded affably and wished them a good day. Just as they were about to pass each other and the man was presumably preparing to ride straight down to Jacksonville to summon help, Dan spoke. He said, 'Say, fella, I wonder if you might help me?'

'Why surely. What's the case?'

'Lookee here,' said Dan and pulled something from his pocket, as though to show the man. Then, as the rider moved towards him, Fraser dropped the coin that he had pulled from his pocket and drew an enormous Bowie knife from the sheath which held it. This was fastened at the back of his pants, threaded through his belt and hidden from view by his jacket. As soon as he caught sight of the blade, the man tried to back off; only to find Seth's horse blocking his retreat. As he fully realized his peril and was on the point of pulling his pistol, Dan launched himself from the saddle and grabbed hold of the man. They both fell to the ground, struggling.

As soon as the fight began, Seth Fraser dismounted and began kicking viciously at the fellow's head, every time it came into range. As soon as the man was sufficiently stunned, Dan grabbed hold of his hair, yanked back his head and cut his throat, as neatly as though he were slaughtering a hog. The murder took less than ten seconds from the moment when Dan Fraser first spoke. He and his brother worked well as a team, hardly needing to say anything to each other beforehand about their plans;

they understood each other that well.

The horse presented them with a problem. It was easy enough to bundle the man's corpse behind the trees, where, with luck, it would lay concealed for a week or two. The horse was a different matter entirely. Even if they killed it, a dead horse invites questions and is too large to hide with any facility. In the end, they decided to take it back to the house with them.

None of this had been marked by either of the other two men watching the farm. The one on the rise of ground saw the Frasers turn into the track leading to their farm and observed that they were leading a riderless horse. He waited until he was sure that neither man would catch sight of him and then wriggled backwards down the slope to his horse. He did not feel that it would be the smart move to ride back to the road and chose instead to lead his horse away on foot and try to cut across the fields to pick up the road a little further north.

As the Frasers entered the yard, Mary-Anne came running up to them, in order to apprise them of the strange and alarming visitors that they had missed. As she chattered on, anxiously eyeing the two brothers for fear that she had acted wrongly, Seth surveyed the land around the farm. His sharp eyes saw the glint of sunlight moving on something in a little copse over half a mile away. He had the vision of a lynx and it had often been the saving of him. While he smiled encouragingly at that stupid little fool of a girl, he tried to gauge what might be causing the winking flashes from the trees.

Somebody signalling by flashing a piece of looking glass? No, the flashes were too irregular for that. A man training a pair of field glasses on him? That was a possibility, except that whatever was causing the light did not appear to be as shiny as glass. In the end, he decided that there was a purposeless and aimless quality about the flashes, which suggested that an animal was involved. From

206

that, it was no great leap of the imagination to think that a horse was moving about restlessly and that some shiny items attached to the bridle or saddle were catching the sunlight intermittently.

What Seth Fraser could see were in fact brightly polished brasses that adorned the saddle of the horse belonging to the fellow who was currently peeping over the wall at the farm. Like most of the men who had come down from Chicago, he liked to make a lot of himself and whereas some went for Spanish saddles or tooled leather, he favoured exotic brasses, which glinted and winked in the sun.

When they had dismissed the girl to her duties, Seth said to his brother, 'Don't stare too particular, but there is a horse standing over in Lone Copse. I reckon it belongs to another of those watchers.

'You mean that yellowish winking?'

'That's it.'

'Well, if that's the horse, where's the rider?'

Larry Davis did not dare now to duck down out of sight below the wall. Both brothers were facing in his direction and he was afraid that any sudden movement might draw their attention to him. So he remained stock still and horribly aware that if anybody were to look closely from the distance that the Frasers were from him, he would be visible. He cursed himself for not ducking down as soon as he saw them ride into the yard.

Seth and Dan sat on their horses, apparently at their ease, looking for all the world like two men just talking of this, that and nothing in particular. Actually, they were scanning their surroundings methodically for anything the least bit out of place. Every so often, one would speak and the other smile or shake his head, but all the while they were looking for the owner of the horse which was standing up in the copse.

At length, Dan said, 'I have him now. He is crouching behind that wall, straight ahead of us. He's got dark hair, which makes it hard to see against them bushes, but if you look a little to the left there, you can see the white of his forehead.'

'Yes, by God,' said Seth, 'I believe you're right. He won't be able to reach his horse, but do you think he'll shoot if we ride at him?'

'I don't know that we've a choice. We can't let him get away.'

'You're right. What shall it be then, guns out and gallop at him?'

'Yes,' said Dan, 'and there's no time like the present.'

The two of them spurred their horses on and set off straight at the man crouching behind the wall. Davis knew that he had been spotted; he jumped to his feet and began sprinting towards where he had left his horse. He didn't believe that he was going to make it in time and he was perfectly correct.

The Frasers worked like pack hunters. Seth rode on ahead of the man, to get between him and his mount, while

Dan moved in from behind, pistol on hand and waiting until he could rein in and get a good shot at his quarry. Larry Davis, though, had been in a good many tight spots before and was not about to roll over and die for this pair of villains. He wasn't going to be able to make it to the trees where his horse was waiting, but that didn't mean that he was finished yet.

As he ran, Davis drew his own piece and without stopping, snapped off a shot over his shoulder in the general direction of Dan Fraser. It didn't hit him, but caused Fraser to duck down and jink to the side. The running man had seen that there were bushes and undergrowth to his right and he dived into this and then dropped to his hands and knees. This unexpected move threw the Frasers for a moment and because Davis had the sense to remain dead still and not to go scuttling off further into the undergrowth, there was no clue as to where he might be hidden; other than that they had seen where he entered the area.

There was now an added sense of urgency to the hunt, because of the shot that the man had fired. There was no telling if anybody had heard that or if others would take it as a sign to move in and surround their house. It was no time for subtlety and so the two men rode together at speed into the bushes, their horses trampling them as they went. The animals weren't too keen on this and had to be urged on constantly by kicks and vigorous prods from spurs.

Horses are sensitive beasts and often sense the presence of other animals long before a man will be aware of them. In this instance, Seth's horse reared and bucked, not wanting to tread on something in front of him. Larry Davis, although as cold-blooded as they come, did not take to the idea of being trampled to death by a couple of horses and so broke cover. Before standing up, though, he fired twice towards the horses and their riders. At that range, he could scarcely miss and

Seth's horse gave a pitiful whinny, reared once more and then jerked convulsively, before falling sideways, mortally wounded. Seth leaped free in time, at the same moment that Dan Fraser drew down on the man who had now shown himself. He fired twice. The first ball took the Pinkertons' agent in the shoulder, but the second passed clean through his skull, blowing out the back of his head.

'There's no time to lose,' said Dan. 'Stop fooling around down there and jump up here. There's two other mounts over in Long Field. We needs must make haste now, uncommon haste. Lord knows who might've heard those shots.'

In fact three people had heard the shooting on the Frasers' place. One was a neighbouring farmer who was not on very intimate terms with the Fraser brothers. He thought that it was no affair of his what was happening there and if either the Frasers were killing somebody or themselves being killed, then it did not concern him. He continued with his work and gave no further thought to it.

The second person who heard the shots was the Pinkertons' agent who had marked the brothers arriving home and had then set off back to Jacksonville. He had tried to take a short cut to the road, avoiding the vicinity of the Frasers' farmhouse in the process. They say that short cuts make for long delays and that was definitely the case with this particular short cut. The man would have sworn on his life that he could reach the road by a short detour round the back of the little hillock upon which he had been perched. Fifteen minutes later, though, and he was stuck in a boggy patch of ground where a stream swollen by the spring rains had overflowed and flooded the land. When he heard the shooting start, he knew that he had to move fast and that probably mean retracing his steps and joining the road by the Frasers' house after all.

The final person to hear the shooting

which showed that the Fraser brothers were in action was Dale Carnak. The shots jerked him out of his sleep and for a moment he could not recollect where he was. Then he remembered that he was in the barn nigh to the Fraser brothers' home and that his intent was to take them into Jacksonville as his prisoners. He stood up and then checked the scattergun. Sometimes, the copper percussion caps would fall from the nipples if they were not a snug fit, but both were still in place.

Carnak looked cautiously through the little door at the front of the hay loft and saw Seth and Dan, both mounted on the same horse and galloping towards the house. He climbed down the ladder to where his horse was waiting patiently below.

12

When they entered the house, the first sound the Frasers heard was the imperious rapping of their mother's cane on the floor above their heads. Mary-Anne had been terrified out of her wits by the gunfire and was crouched in a corner of the kitchen, sobbing, with her apron pulled over her head. The two brothers knew that they needed to move very fast, but even so, they could not ignore their ma's summons. Besides which, they owed her some few words of explanation for the way in which they were about to light out.

When they went into their mother's room, it was plain at once that the old lady knew something was amiss. 'What's all that shooting?' she asked and then immediately said, 'no, don't tell me. Some murder or other, I've no doubt.'

'Ma,' said Seth, who had always been

more favoured by his mother than Dan, 'Ma, we have to take a little trip. I hope it won't be for long.'

'In short, the two of you are in a fix and have to go on the run. It's just as I always knew things would come to. You're a rare couple of boys. You always was. Why couldn't I have had girls instead? Boys surely are a trial and a torment.'

'We can't delay, Ma. There might be men come looking for us.'

'Yes, I know all about that. That Orville Larssen, nasty weaselly fellow, was here with some others.'

'So Mary-Anne gave us to understand,' said Dan. 'She's down in the kitchen now, having a fit of the vapours.'

'Those men don't count,' said their mother, ignoring Dan, 'You'll escape them. It's that other you need to heed.'

'What other?' asked Seth.

'Young man. Very polite and meek. You might think butter wouldn't melt in his mouth. I weren't taken in. I tell you boys now, that fellow will be the death of you 'less you stay sharp as you always were. He's the one to watch out for. Never you mind Larssen and those others.'

Their mother spoke as though she could in truth see the future and observe their doings from afar and Seth shivered suddenly, like somebody had walked over his grave. He said quietly to his brother, 'She means Carnak, damn him.'

'I've a bag here with enough cash money to keep you going for a spell,' said Mrs Fraser, beckoning the brothers closer to her bed. 'Here now, take it and be off with you. Like as not somebody has heard those shots. If an old cripple like me hears them and asks what's to do, then likely enough there'll be others.'

Seth and Dan kissed their mother awkwardly; they were not a family much given to displays of affection. Seth said, 'There's nothing really against us Ma, only suspicion. Happen we'll be able to come back in six, maybe nine months.'

'Whether or no, I'll not see the pair of you again,' said the old woman with absolute assurance, as though some foreknowledge was upon her. 'Either I'll die or you two will. It makes no odds which, this is goodbye for good and all. You get on now or you'll be caught for sure.'

As they went to their rooms to gather a few belongings, Seth said, 'That Carnak. To think he was in her room there, disturbing her. I could hope that we do meet, so's I can kill him.'

'Or him you,' said Dan. 'Did you not hear what Ma said?'

It took the two men only five minutes to ransack their rooms and throw what was needful into leather saddle-bags. They went down to the kitchen and while Seth went to call in one of the horses from Long Field, his brother put together a few provisions. After he had brought the horse into the yard, Seth went over to the barn to fetch the tack. As soon as he entered the rickety old wooden structure, Seth had the strangest feeling, as though somebody had just left. He even thought that his nostrils could detect the faintest trace of horse in the air. But that was crazy; they didn't bring their mounts into the barn to tack up.

Seth Fraser stood there for a moment, the hairs on the back of his neck bristling, as they sometimes did when he was in danger. He looked round once more, but could see nothing out of place. He was getting spooked by what his ma had said. He knew well enough that she wasn't really a witch, but there were times when she talked like she knew more than other folks about the future. He shook his head. It was all a lot of foolishness.

When he had tacked up the bay, Seth went back into the kitchen to say a final few words to the servant girl. 'Listen up now, Mary-Anne,' he told her, firmly but not unkindly, 'the others, meaning the hired helps, will be back this afternoon. You tell them what chanced here today. You hear what I tell you?'

'Yes, sir,' said the frightened girl, 'I hear you.'

'Mind you tell Rene the truth, him in especial. He knows what to do and will see to things. You won't run out and leave your mistress helpless, will you?'

'Oh no,' said the girl, shocked that he would think her capable of such a thing. 'Mrs Fraser, she has always been good to me, taking me from the orphans' asylum and training me and such. I wouldn't leave her now.'

'There's a good girl,' said Seth, 'I knew you'd stick by her.'

'Hark,' said Dan, 'You hear hoofs?'

They listened and all three heard the sound of hoof beats, but they were receding, rather than approaching. It was the last surviving Pinkerton's man who had finally found his way back to the road and was now making all due haste for Jacksonville.

'I wouldn't be far from the mark,' said Seth, 'were I to guess that that's another of those devils gone rushing off to town to raise the alarm that we have come back.'

'Come on,' said his brother, 'we still

have time in hand. We'll make it yet.'

The two men went out into the yard and mounted their horses. Then, with no more ado, they set off at a canter down the short driveway to the road. When they reached it, Seth said to his brother, 'Which way?'

'Well,' replied Dan, laughing, 'I don't quite fancy the road north. I reckon it must be south and away from Jacksonville.'

Strange to relate, neither of the Frasers were feeling too bad about the way things had ended up. They were tolerably sure of being able to make a living for as long as it took for the heat to die down at the farm. They knew that Rene, one of the hands, would be able to keep them in touch with developments, as he had in the past when they had left home for a while. Life became a little stale after a time, living on the farm with their mother. It might be a little lively and restore their appetite for life to live on the road for a bit.

The road ahead of them turned sharply, almost in a right angle, to avoid an outcrop of rocks. This section of the way also dipped down suddenly and the consequence was that you were unable to see around that corner until you had actually passed along the road. Seth and Dan Fraser cantered along the road, not wasting time, but neither galloping flat out. They had to slow as the road turned to the left and as they brought their mounts into a trot and swung round the bend, they saw a rider planted squarely in the middle of the road ahead, quite plainly holding it against them. This man had a doubled-barrelled scattergun of antique appearance at his shoulder and aimed straight at them. They reined in twenty feet from this menacing figure.

'Hidy,' said Dale Carnak. 'I was hoping you boys would drop by.'

Both Seth and Dan had made the calculation that since that gun was cocked and Carnak had almost certainly taken first pull upon the trigger, it would be suicide to go for their pistols. They waited to see what he would say next. They hadn't long to wait, because as soon as he saw that they had weighed up the pros and cons of the situation correctly, the young man said, 'You unbuckle those gun-belts. Real slow, mind, because I am already pressing the trigger and if I make a mistake now, then we shan't be able to put it right in this world. Slowly does it, now.'

As they undid their belts, Carnak said, 'Then you drop them in the road. When you've done that, pull those carbines from their scabbards and throw them down as well.'

When they had done so, Dan said, 'What now, you young bastard?'

'Now?' asked Carnak in surprise, 'Now you dismount and we start back to town. I said I'd bring the two of you in and that is just what I am aiming for to do.'

'You are one yellow bastard,' said Seth. 'Were you a real man, you would face off to us, man to man.'

Carnak laughed out loud at that. 'I

don't need to prove I'm a man,' he said, shaking his head, 'I proved that in the war. Was you two fighting?' When neither of the brothers replied, he said, 'Yes, just like I guessed, you dodged the column. Too busy stealing and killing to serve your country, I guess. Get down off them horses.'

The brothers climbed down and then Dan said, 'Still and all, you durst not face me in a fair fight. You know it to be true. You talk big when you got the drop on me, but you'd be singing a different tune if we both had pistols at our hips and was standing facing each other.'

Carnak said nothing. This was because he felt that Dan Fraser had a point. There was something a little unmanly about bracing a fellow in this wise when one held a shotgun and the other was defenceless. He said, 'You two stand away from those guns, I will come down.' Having said this, he dismounted, all the whole time keeping the scattergun trained on the two of them.

When he reached the ground, he picked up one of the gun-belts and, setting his own gun against the rocks, buckled it on; all the while, never taking his eyes from the Frasers. He knew that he was acting like a mad fool, but the accusation of cowardice had got beneath his hide like a cockleburr.

'Here's what we will do,' he said. 'First off is where you, Seth, can sit down there to my right. Then your brother can put on the other gun-belt and we will see who is afeared to face who on equal terms. Seth, you can call.'

While saying this and as Dan came over and picked up the gun-belt, Carnak never once took his eyes off either of the brothers for a second. He knew they were as fast as rattlesnakes and slippery as eels and he had a feeling that despite the appeal to his honour, they would both of them shoot him in the back if the opportunity presented itself.

When Dan had fastened on the rig and had a holster hanging at his hip, Carnak said, 'If you will face up to me now in a fair fight, then why not back over there slowly and take your stand where you will. Then, when you stop, let your brother give a signal, by calling 'go' or something of that sort.'

'So be it,' said Dan Fraser, ''Go' it shall be. You agree, Seth?'

'I'm ready when you are,' said his brother, 'only, hurry up and kill this cowson, so that we can be on our way. Time is pressing.'

As Dan Fraser walked slowly backwards, Carnak could not help but feel that he had taken a wrong turn. These men were professionals; for them shooting and killing were second nature. True, he had killed plenty of men in the war, but he had never acquired what you might call a taste for it, seeing killing a fellow human being more as a sometimes unavoidable necessity, rather than a desirable way of life.

Then there was no longer time to think on such things, because Dan Fraser had stopped moving and was standing twenty-five feet away and staring at Carnak with an expression of pure hatred on his face. If ever in his life, either during or after the war, Carnak had seen a determination in a man's face to end his life, this was that moment.

In fact, Dan Fraser was far faster than Dale Carnak and if the contest had been fair, then he would without any doubt at all have laid Carnak in his grave. The two men were focused with every fibre of their being upon each other, both dead set on killing the other, sooner than being killed himself. That was why they neither of them noticed Seth bringing up his legs so that instead of sitting, he was crouching with his legs under him; ready to spring.

As he cried 'Go!', Seth leaped up and made a dive for the scattergun, where it was resting against a boulder. The streak of movement off to the side of him, took Dan by surprise and caused him to take his eyes off Carnak for a fraction of a second, even as his hand was snaking down for the pistol.

Carnak, who had expected some treachery from one or the other of the brothers, was not taken aback by Seth's attempt to seize the shotgun. He fired twice at Dan Fraser, before Fraser's gun was even level, and then jumped at Seth, cracking him round the head with the pistol and so causing him to relinquish his hold on the gun. To be on the safe side, Carnak pistol whipped the man into submission, not ceasing until Seth Fraser was lying stunned in the road.

He then went over to check on Dan, who was, as he had supposed, stone dead. The crazy thing was that he probably would not have had a chance of firing first if both the brothers had played fair. They had brought this down upon themselves.

Seth was groaning and showing signs of raising his head. Carnak toyed with the idea of putting a ball through the devil's brain, but decided that he should bring at least one of the men in alive.

As he stood there, Carnak heard the rumble of a considerable body of riders, heading in his direction. Whoever they were, they stopped and he guessed that they had been heading along the road from Jacksonville towards the Frasers' farm. He picked up the scattergun and used it to cover Seth, who was now on all fours, retching and groaning. The riders had set off again and Carnak supposed that they had heard that the Frasers had not long left their farm and since they had not met them on the road north, must have assumed that they had come this way. Carnak didn't know how he stood with either the sheriff or Pinkertons, but he supposed that he would soon find out.

The body of horseman slowed as they reached the bend in the road and then there were cries from those in front to halt, when they saw the scene before them.

Nobody called for Carnak to throw down his weapon, which he had at first expected. He kept it pointed at Seth

Fraser, because he still didn't trust him not to stage a miraculous recovery. The sheriff, who was in the lead of the riders, said, 'You seem to have done our job for us. You would be Dale Carnak, unless I am much mistook.'

'You ain't mistook. Carnak's my name all right.'

'Is that Dan Fraser I see lying over yonder? Is he dead?'

'We fought fair and I killed him. His brother here tried a trick and I have subdued him. You can take him now.'

Pete Relph said, 'We have been looking for you for some little time, Mr Carnak. Our boss is most desirous of seeing you at our office in Chicago. I think that after this, he will be wanting to congratulate you. It is the neatest job I ever saw and one of them left alive as well. Well done.'

'I ain't suspected or wanted for anything?' asked Carnak, hardly able to believe it.

'Not by me,' said Larssen, 'except to relieve you of those cuffs. Mind telling me how you managed to part 'em in that way?'

'Fellow called Jethro did it for me with his axe. This here's his gun.'

'That old rascal,' said Sheriff Larssen. 'I'll bet he couldn't wait to help a fellow wrongdoer, as he saw the case. Come over here, Mr Carnak and I'll set you free of the other bits.'

Carnak went over to the sheriff, who produced a key and unlocked the cuffs which still encircled his wrists. 'Why, that surely is a great relief,' said Carnak. 'You don't get used to such things, no matter how long you're wearing them.'

Seth Fraser had come to now and was rising groggily to his feet. Larssen said to him, 'Seth, I'm sorry to tell you that you are under arrest on suspicion of murder.' He dismounted and produced another pair of handcuffs. 'You ain't going to give me no trouble, I suppose?'

'We nearly made it,' said Fraser. 'Woulda done too if not for that young son of a bitch. I knew he was trouble, for all that I owe him my life. He saved my life and now I think he's taken it away again. Don't tell me, Orville, I know this here is a hanging matter.'

After he was securely cuffed and mounted on his horse, amid the Pinkertons' riders, he spoke once more. 'Don't be letting my brother's body lie there in the dirt. It is the hell of a thing to see your own brother shot down like that in front of you.'

Carnak said, 'It most likely wouldn't've happened had you not gone for the gun. I reckon your brother could've beat me in a fair duel.'

'He could've beat you for sure,' said Fraser, 'which makes it all the bitterer that I was the cause of his death and not you.'

13

The special edition of *The Jacksonville and Bartlow County Intelligencer and Weekly Record* for 18 April carried a banner headline, declaring, 'Local Businessman in Gaol; Suspected of being Train Robber.' Beneath this was a piece which the editor himself wrote, thinking it very stylish and good enough for the *New York Times*:

They say that truth is stranger than fiction and the veracity of this wise old saw was amply demonstrated on the 14th inst. when SETH FRASER, the well known local entrepreneur was arrested on a charge of multiple murder. It will be recalled by our readers, that two weeks since, we reported a curious little incident when an out-of-towner named DALE CARNAK saved Mr FRASER from certain death by knocking aside the arm of a would-be assassin. In an extraordinary twist of fate, it was this same DALE CARNAK who later apprehended Mr FRASER on the capital charge. It seems that appearances can, as is widely claimed, be deceptive, and rather than the drifter for which many took him to be, this same Mr CARNAK is in truth none other than an agent of the PINK-ERTONS DETECTIVE AGENCY in CHICAGO. Mr CARNAK has now returned to the metropolis to continue his duties with the famous detective agency. It is an amazing circumstance that Mr CARNAK should begin his visit to JACKSONVILLE by saving SETH FRASER's life and end it by setting him in peril of being hanged.

It was not every new recruit to Pinkertons who was welcomed personally into the organization by the great man himself, but Alan Pinkerton had expressed the desire to see young Carnak as soon as he arrived in Chicago. He still felt a little guilty for having wished the young man ill and so seeing Dale Carnak and being effusive in his greeting was a means of salving his own conscience.

'So ye're the young fellow as caused us so much trouble? I'm vairy, vairy glad to see ye, m'boy. I hope that ye'll enjoy working with us here and make a name for yeself. Not but that ye've already begun. Taking those rascals single handed now, that took pluck.'

Carnak was somewhat overwhelmed by this great flow of words from such a famous personage and mumbled some inaudible reply. Shooting and such lively action was one thing, but fancy words had never been his style. Alan Pinkerton gripped Carnak's hand in his own meaty paw and shook it heartily, saying, 'Welcome, my boy, to the Pinkertons Detective Agency.'

Other titles in the
Linford Western Library:

THE KILLING DAYS

Neil Hunter

Corruption is running rampant between members of government and powerful businessmen: bribery, conspiracy, and illegal dealings. Henry Quinlan, sent by Senator Howard Beauchamp to investigate, patiently compiled a dossier of evidence against the culprits. When he dispatched his documentation to the senator by train, protected by two Pinkerton detectives, it was stolen en route — and Quinlan disappeared. Now Jason Brand has been called in to track down both the dossier and its author. But someone's determined to stop him . . .

FOOL'S GOLD

Brent Larssen

Bill Tucker has spent most of his life being pushed around. When he moves out to Wyoming and buys his own patch of ground, he is determined not to be seen as a small man anymore. But when he discovers gold on his new acres, he draws the attention of Septimus Arkwright, a local cattle company owner. For, blaming the Homestead Act for bringing Tucker to these parts, Arkwright considers the land — and the gold — to be rightfully his . . .

COUGAR PROWLS

Owen G. Irons

Battle-hardened Carroll Cougar has finally made it home to his little ranch on Twin Creek with his new bride, Ellen, after spending years fighting under General Crook in the Apache Wars. But Cougar and Ellen have left too many enemies alive behind them, and more have accumulated in Twin Creek in their absence. Once more, Cougar must buckle on his guns and go out prowling, until he has defeated every last one of his adversaries.

BULLET CATCH SHOWDOWN

I. J. Parnham

Stage magician Malachi Muldoon is the world's most dangerous practitioner of the arcane arts with his performance of the notorious bullet catch. His show in Bear Creek draws the interest of Adam Clements and Deputy Hayward Knight. While Clements is keen to join Malachi on stage and become part of his act, Hayward is out to try and solve a mystery: it seems that, wherever Malachi Muldoon performs, a trail of bodies is left behind . . .

STEARN'S BREAK

Caleb Rand

Looking to start a new life, away from the futility of working an exhausted gold mine, Will Stearn and his partner Clem Tapper ride to Ragland. On the way, they encounter Connie Boe and her wounded driver, and stop to assist. Accepting Connie's offer of paying them to ride shotgun and guard her wagon the rest of the journey, Will and Clem travel on with the others. But when they reach Ragland, they'll find that the town is tough . . .

THE PLAINSMAN

Steve Hayes and Ben Bridges

After seeing his father set upon and stabbed, nothing will ever be the same for young Will Cody. He kills his first man at the age of ten, and the following years see him fight constant battles — against marauding Cheyenne, the Civil War, the Great Plains themselves, and merciless guerrilla fighters. But even spit-and-grit Will Cody — more famously known as Buffalo Bill — is only human . . . and has he finally met his match?